The Chimes
of Westminster

Books
by Gary W. Priester

Looking Good in Color

Startling Stereograms

Hidden Treasures

Eye Tricks

Eyeball on Fire

Hidden Words

The Chimes
of Westminster

—AND OTHER SHORT STORIES—

Gary W. Priester

TOVAH
MIRIAM

Gary W. Priester

ISBN: 978-0-578-93216-3

First Printing

Printed in USA

Cover Photograph: Mikhail Leonov - ShutterStock

Author Photo: Selfie

Cover and Book Design: gwpriester

www.gwpriester.com

TOVAH
MIRIAM

Little hands moving like lightning.
—Florence Padway

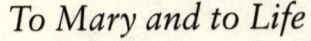

To Mary and to Life

— CONTENTS —

The Chimes
of Westminster

THE CLOCK ARRIVED in a heavy cardboard box. The hand-written return address read, "Arthur Brown, Esq., 1300 East Hancock Avenue, Milwaukee, WI." The box had been left on the front porch by their mail carrier but not their regular carrier. This guy looked like a Gahan Wilson cartoon, like someone from another place and time.

Sid brought the box into the house and set it down on the dining room table. He brought a pair of scissors from the kitchen and cut the transparent packing tape.

Beth, Sid's wife of forty-three years, looked on as Sid opened the box and took out a letter addressed to him.

The letter simply said that Sid's Great Aunt Florence Jacobs had died at the age of ninety-one and had expressed a desire for Sid to have the enclosed clock, a family heirloom. The letter was signed by Arthur Brown, Esq., executor of the estate of Sid's deceased great aunt.

After Sid removed all of the packing materials, an antique mahogany bracket clock was revealed and a small envelope that contained a key, attached to a ribbon, for winding the clock.

The clock had a well-worn, practical, silver face with simple hands, simple Arabic numbers, and three holes for winding the clock. The wear around the winding holes indicated the clock had seen much use. There were small, curved arrows above each of the holes to indicate the direction each gear should be wound. The top of the case was arched, typical of bracket clocks, and was topped with a brass handle. The wooden case gave off an evocative wood smell from generations of use. The face displayed the name C. G. Gowland which was printed under the number 12, and at the bottom, the name Sunderland was printed just above the 6. Above the numbers on the face were two small dials that could be adjusted by hand, one that read "Silent and Chime," and the other was a dial for regulating the speed of the clock.

Sid wound each of the three separate winding mechanisms, being careful not to overwind. Then referring to the exact time on his cell phone, he rotated the big hand to set the correct time. When the big hand passed 3, the clock made a whirring sound and then chimed a few notes that sounded familiar. At 6 and 9 there was also a chiming that increased in complexity. Finally, as the large hand passed 12, the clock chimed what Sid now recognized were the Chimes of Westminster.

...

"That's a beautiful clock," said Beth. "And the chimes are lovely. It's a very impressive legacy."

Sid agreed.

Together they auditioned places in the house where the clock would fit into their eclectic furnishings. After trying several rooms, they decided it should go on the demilune console table in the living room from where it could be heard throughout the small house. The old clock looked right at home on top of the console table.

...

Sid and Beth, now in their seventies, had been slowly losing their hearing for many years, but each in a different range. Beth had difficulty hearing sounds in the higher registers while Sid had more trouble with the middle registers. And if there was any gray noise, such as the forced air heater, or the shower, or a room full of people talking, then Sid's hearing was almost nil.

So when Beth and Sid were lying in bed at night, the sound of the chimes was altered by the many surfaces off which they bounced. Some of the chime notes sounded dull while others sounded bright and tinny. And each spouse heard something slightly different. But hearing the comforting chimes, even when altered, marked the passing of the hours, if only subliminally.

After several months, Beth and Sid almost stopped hearing the chimes. The same way they did not hear the heater go on and off in the winter or the jet planes in the sky over the house. Until one night.

...

It was Beth who, sometime about 3 AM, thought she heard the chimes play "Mary Had A Little Lamb" instead of the Westminster Chimes melody. She said, "Sid? Did you hear that?" Sid, who was out like a light, said nothing. Staying awake for the next several hours, Beth heard only the Westminster Chimes. Finally, exhausted, sure that she must have been dreaming, she fell asleep.

Weeks passed without event, and the aberrant chime was forgotten. But then it was Sid's turn. After a stressful few days, Sid had been lying awake for several hours unable to sleep. At 1 AM Sid heard the chimes play the opening notes from the Beatle's song "Hey Jude." "Nah," he thought. "I must have been dreaming." Beth, lying beside him, was asleep, breathing softly, as were their two cats, Heather and Leslie, at the foot of the bed.

Sid mentioned the 1 AM chimes to Beth the next morning when they were having their coffee. But neither gave it a second thought and chalked it up to fatigue and their collective hearing loss.

...

Summer had come and, as they had done for every summer since moving to New Mexico in 2001, Sid and Beth were sitting with glasses of wine — red for Sid, white for Beth — on their west-facing deck as the setting sun was producing yet another intensely colorful sunset. With the windows and the screen door open, they could hear the reassuring chiming of the clock in the living room as it sounded the 8 PM half hour. All was quiet except for the sound of crickets and a coyote in the distance. Sid got up and looked over the deck railing down into the arroyo. It was a sharp decline that could easily give one vertigo.

Sid had been "mansplaining" the recent election and what Sid thought it meant to their financial future. Beth, who did the bookkeeping and was better with numbers than Sid, was agreeing. The economy would undoubtedly be good for their portfolio.

They were both engrossed in the subject of the markets, and so they almost did not notice when the clock, chiming 9 PM, left out the Westminster Chimes and just struck the hour nine times. Then as an afterthought, the clock chimed what sounded like "If I Were a Rich Man," the song from *Fiddler on the Roof*.

"There is something not kosher about this clock, Beth," Sid said. Beth agreed.

...

"I didn't really know Aunt Florence very well," Sid said. "I only met her once when I was in my teens, and she came to visit us for a week. I do remember that she seemed a bit off but in an endearing sort of way. Maybe this clock is some kind of joke from the grave?"

...

The following day, Sid needed to run some errands in Albuquerque, and he took the clock with him. He stopped at the only clock shop in town that actually had a trained clockmaker. He explained the quirkiness of the clock and asked the owner, Matt, if he could have a look and maybe stop the clock from making mischief. Matt said it would be a few weeks before he could look at the clock, but he promised to call Sid with the results as soon as he had something to report.

Over the next few days, while the clock was at the clock shop, Sid did some online research on clocks, specifically his bracket clock. He learned that the clock was made in the Victorian era by C. G. Gowland of Sunderland, England. Digging deeper into his research, he discovered that the clockmaker who had built this specific clock was a German gentleman named Hans Deitler, who, before moving with his family to England, had done his apprenticeship at Badische Uhrenfabrik, an old and respected German clockmaker.

Shortly after arriving in England, Hans Deitler's wife, Gretchen, left Hans for a tradesman who went door to door sharpening knives. She took their five-year-old daughter, Monique, and the family dachshund, Fritz, with her. Curiously, it was the dog that Hans missed most.

Digging even deeper, Sid found an obscure website, antiqueclockschmutz.net, that confirmed the details Sid's research had already turned up. It also added to the information Sid had found that Hans and Gretchen eventually did divorce, and Gretchen married the knife sharpener. They remained on good terms, and Gretchen allowed Hans visitation rights. He frequently came by and took Fritz out for a walk.

As a show of magnanimity, Hans gave the newlyweds a bracket clock. Possibly even the same one that was bequeathed to Sid by Great Aunt Florence. All this information Syd shared with Beth, who was intrigued and impressed at the provenance of the mysterious bracket clock. The article went on, but apparently Sid missed the part about Gretchen's nervous breakdown, or, if he had read that part, it failed to register.

...

A month or so later, Sid received a phone call from Matt, who said he had taken the clock completely apart, cleaned and oiled all the parts, and reassembled them. Matt certified the clock to be in excellent condition. He also added that there was an odd gear assembly that really had nothing to do with the clock's function, and he had removed it. This gear assembly might have been some kind of practical joke that Herr Deitler built into the clock to annoy his ex-wife and Trevor, the sharpener of knives, her new husband. But Matt could not explain the clock's knowing "Hey Jude." On their next trip into Albuquerque, Sid and Beth combined lunch, a quick trip to Trader Joe's, and a stop at the clock shop to retrieve their clock.

...

For the next several months — it was by now late spring — the clock behaved admirably. Matt had regulated the clock, and it was only about twenty seconds fast. Life returned to normal, and the clock and the melodious chimes of Westminster just blended into the sounds of everyday living.

Then after one Friday night dinner, a bottle of wine, and streaming several episodes from Season 3 of *The Crown* Sid and Beth turned in for the night. The last episode they had watched focused on the queen's husband, Prince Philip, the Duke of Edinburgh. Sometime around 3 AM or 4 AM, the clock chimed "Rule Britannia." And this time they both heard it. "So much for Matt's fixing the clock," Sid mused.

Over the next few weeks, Beth and Sid were treated to random snatches of "Deutschlandlied," "Stars and Stripes Forever," "Don't Cry for Me Argentina," "Mr. Sandman," and "A Hard Day's Night." Always in some way related to the streaming content they had watched earlier that night. It was starting to get out of hand. It was no longer cute. It was beginning to feel sinister.

Sid, looking inside the clock, discovered a small lever that he hoped would be the end of their nocturnal concerts. It was marked "Night Shutoff," and it disabled the chimes from 9 PM until 7 AM. And so peace returned to the household. At least at night. But frequently during waking hours, the chimes would crank out something unexpected and not necessarily something pleasant.

...

It was January, and Sid was turning seventy-five. Beth thought a party was in order. She invited a group of close friends and neighbors for a festive birthday brunch. Beth had not really cooked anything from scratch for years. She frequently joked, "I no longer cook. I heat." So she made the affair pot luck. "We'll supply the drinks if you supply the food," she texted the invitees. Interest in attending Sid's party was high because by now the antics of Great Aunt Florence's aberrant timepiece were common knowledge.

Beth was wondering which clock would show up tomorrow, the one that played the lovely Westminster Chimes, or the mischievous clock that liked to surprise. Either way it would be entertaining, and they *would* find out tomorrow. Beth's best guess was it would be the naughty clock.

In all, there were sixteen people bringing food, and beer, and wine, to celebrate Sid's Diamond Birthday. It was a happy and festive event, and a good time was had by all. Sadly, or maybe not, the clock stuck to the program and played only the Chimes of Westminster. After a few hours, the clock was forgotten, and everyone just had a good time socializing and catching up on the latest gossip.

The last guests departed around 7 PM and Beth volunteered to do the washing up because it was Sid's birthday. Afterwards they sat by the remains of the fire in companionable silence with the last of the coffee. By then it was past 9 PM, and the chimes had shut off for the night.

...

As Sid was turning off the lights in the living room, and they both were looking forward to crawling into bed, the mute clock chimed the first five notes of "Happy Birthday to YOU!" They groaned in unison. With the half-hour, three-quarter hour, and at 10 PM, the chimes worked their way up to a full chorus of "Happy Birthday to You."

But the clock was not finished. For the next hour, it chimed "Happy Birthday to You" continuously, stopping just long enough for the tired couple to doze off before starting up again. Beth commented it was just like the night from hell when the smoke alarm peeped every three minutes as a reminder the battery was low and needed to be replaced, and they were out of the proper batteries.

Sid sat up in bed and shouted, "ENOUGH!" But the clock was on a mission and would not stop. Sid got up, opened the bezel, and turned the small dial from "CHIME" to "SILENT." And for a blessed half hour, the clock was silent. But at 11:15 PM it started up again.

Sid got out of bed, walked into the living room, picked up the clock — still chiming — and carried it out onto the living room deck, the deck that overlooked the deep arroyo. "Forgive me, Aunt Florence, but this has gone far enough." And with a loud grunt, he flung the clock over the railing and onto the steep hillside, where it landed on a big rock, ricocheted off the rock, and rolled, hitting one rock after another until it came to rest at the bottom of the arroyo with the case smashed and a path of gears and springs in its wake. Beth, who had followed Sid onto the deck, breathed a sigh of relief as what remained of the clock came to a rest and one final discordant chime was heard.

And then peace. Blessed peace. Sanity-restoring peace.

The exhausted couple climbed back into bed and, just as they were dozing off to sleep, the toilet flushed.

All by itself.

The Family Shetetl

─────────⊙─────────

I GREW UP IN THE EARLY 1940s in the small, affluent, hillside community of Laurel Hills in sunny Southern California. Most of the homes were mansion-sized with lush tropical landscaping and Mediterranean design with arched doorways and red tile roofs. The residential streets were wide and lined with palm trees. Many famous movie stars lived in the neighborhood. And many other wealthy and important people from the movie industry lived there as well.

And then there was my family.

We lived on the other side of the tracks in what my rabbi jokingly called, "the family shtetl": two twelve-unit apartment buildings. The family shtetl reference was because at one time, out of twenty-four apartments, six were occupied by members of my family.

We shared the same telephone prefix with the rich and famous — ours was Crestview 52620 — but they lived in gorgeous homes while we lived in "units." Ironically, I later found out that many of the fabulous homes were mortgaged to the hilt. One paycheck away from foreclosure.

Appearances can be deceptive.

Our apartments were unencumbered with debt. They were fully paid for. And I might add, profitable. So you might be wondering how my family came to be landlords.

...

It all started in the country of Lithuania, a country that is now part of the Baltic states. But when my Grandmother, Leva, was a child, Lithuania belonged to Russia. My grandmother used to tell me stories of the small village where she grew up. Her father was a shopkeeper, and the family almost always had food on the table. But they lived in fear of the Cossacks, the equivalent of today's motorcycle gangs. The Cossacks were militant Christians who rode enormous horses. They wore large fur hats and had sashes across their chests, and they carried long curved swords. And as I understand it, they used those swords with wild abandon. Maybe "terrorists" would be a better description.

If the Cossacks ever came into my great-grandfather's shop — the family was Jewish — they would more than likely destroy the place. Maybe rape the women, and kill the men, and kidnap the children. And they would leave without paying their bill. Because they were Cossacks. It's what they did. You might say, it was their job!

...

The details are sketchy, but when my grandmother was coming of age, the family decided to send Leva, sister Ruth, and their brother, Walter, to live in Germany. In the late 1800s, this was not such a bad idea. But Germany, even in the late 1800s, was not the safest place for Jews to live. And so, my grandmother and her brother and sister escaped from Germany and came to live in Leeds, England, in 1903.

According to my grandmother, no sooner did she, and Ruth, and Walter get off the boat than she was aggressively pursued by an eager young Englishman who would not leave her alone until she agreed to marry him. He appeared to have money and was not at all bad looking. In fact, again I only have my grandmother's word on this, he was enormously handsome, so how could she say no?

Well, she didn't say no. She said, "YES!" And hence became, Mrs. Bernard Stapleton.

The couple was married in in a synagogue in a lavish ceremony and not long after moved to Milwaukee, Wisconsin, in the United States of America. Brother Walter and sister Ruth came along and settled in Milwaukee as well.

...

In Milwaukee, Bernard Stapleton founded a bank with money he had inherited from his family. The bank prospered, and my grandfather's fortunes increased. The venture earned enough money for Bernard to sell the bank and retire at age thirty-five. He and Leva said adieu to the bitterly cold winters and hot stifling summers of Wisconsin and said hello to the year-round summers of sunny Southern California.

My grandfather built a large home —well, he designed the house, a contractor did the actual building — with tennis courts and a very large swimming pool, the site of many lavish parties. The Englishman and his Lithuanian bride blended in well and got to know all their neighbors, all of whom had also moved to Laurel Hills from somewhere else. Their friends included movie stars, bankers, industrialists, and other movers and shakers who had gravitated to this quiet, exclusive, hillside community. And into this home were born my mother and her brother and sister. My mother was the youngest, and her sister was the oldest.

...

Aside from building new homes and public buildings, which he did from time to time to keep his hand in, as he liked to say, Bernard Stapleton was now a man of leisure. And as a new member of the leisure class, Bernard took up traveling. He wanted to see the world. Leva, who had had enough traveling to last a lifetime, opted to stay home, and run the household, and raise her three children.

She also joined the Laurel Hills Women's Club, where in time, she became its president. Life was good, and she had no complaints.

...

One year, when my mom and her siblings were almost in their teens, Bernard Stapleton announced he was soon to embark on a cruise around the world. He would be gone for six months. He had booked a first-class suite and invited my grandmother to join him. This was a formality because, as he knew she would, she declined, saying she was too busy with her duties at the women's club, running the household, and caring for the children.

...

Six months later, my grandfather, looking like a new man, returned from his world cruise bearing gifts for everyone and he regaled one and all with lengthy descriptions of the ports of call, the food, the POSH accommodations, and the shipboard gossip. ("Schmutz," was the word he used to describe the gossip.) He told each and every member of the family how terribly he missed them all and how he could not wait to get home

....

Shortly after Bernard's jubilant return, my grandmother formally welcomed a new member to the Laurel Hills Women's Club. It was right after the monthly meeting when all the members were gathered, and chatting, and drinking cups of coffee from china cups, and snacking on fresh fruit and French pastries.

"I'm Leva Stapleton, the president of the Laurel Hills Women's Club, and I would like to extend our warmest welcome," said my grandmother to the new member.

The new member paused, looking confused. She began to speak, but before she could start, my grandmother continued, "We moved here seventeen years ago from Milwaukee. That's in Wisconsin. We came to the United States from England, where my husband said he would kill himself if I did not marry him. He was such a romantic!"

The new member, who was around the same age as my grandmother, stylishly dressed, with graying hair and lovely hazel eyes, again started to speak but, once again, was cut short by my grandmother.

"My husband, Bernard Stapleton," my grandmother continued, "sold the bank he had founded and retired at thirty-five! We moved here to Laurel Hills and built a big house. You must come to one of our famous pool parties!" The new member's eyes widened. She nodded acknowledgement and once more attempted to speak, only to be cut off yet again by my grandmother.

"But soon, Bernard was bored with retirement and playing tennis every day. He has a financial advisor who invests our money and does very well, I might add. But Bernard is not a reader, he doesn't like to garden, local politics bore him, and so aside from designing new buildings, which he does just to keep busy, traveling to exotic places has become his new hobby. His passion, you might say."

...

Finally, my grandmother paused a second to catch her breath, just long enough for the new member to say, "What an amazing coincidence, Leva. My husband and I met a Bernard Stapleton and his wife on the world cruise we just returned from. At first we thought he was travelling with his daughter, she was so much younger than he was, then he introduced her as his wife! Newlyweds I suspected from the way they behaved. It was shameless really! Everybody at the captain's table was talking about the 'Newlyweds'."

···

The Stapleton's divorce followed shortly thereafter, and the judge awarded my grandmother a very generous settlement, including two brand-new apartment buildings that my grandfather had just built.

Karma, Again

FOR MOST OF HIS ADULT LIFE, Jake had believed in karma. Simply stated, what goes 'round comes 'round, or how you live this life will affect what you will become in your next. To be honest, Jake did not know much about the origins of karma or even how it was supposed to work. He simply believed that you don't wish anyone ill even if, in fact, you wished that person great ill. Because to do so, would bring greater ill right back on you. So that was how he saw it. And for good measure, he added hubris to this. Hubris, as Jake understood it, was the sin of extreme pride. To sum up, don't wish ill of others and be modest and thankful for what you have. Not bad for a philosophy of life.

But after a lifetime observing what he saw as evil people living long healthy lives and generous, good-hearted people dying young from terrible diseases, Jake was starting to formulate a new theory of karma: that karma only works on those who believe in it. Ditto, hubris.

To this Jake added a new theory: some people are so vile and despicable that karma would not hold it against you if you slipped up and wished ill on that kind of person.

...

Jake was born and raised in Southern California and developed a sense of fair play from his liberal parents. He was taught to be tolerant of others and grateful for what he had. His parents taught him that poor people did not aspire to be poor and, if given the opportunity, would work hard to make life better for themselves, their children, and their children's children. "There but for fortune . . ." was the mantra he heard all during his formative years. And so, with an upbringing like that, it is not surprising he embraced both karma and hubris.

He recycled as much as possible, preferred organic food whenever there was a choice, carried his own canvas bags to the market, and tried to leave as small a footprint on the earth as possible. He rode his bicycle two miles to work every day, even in the rain. And he volunteered on weekends at the local food kitchen, cheerfully serving hot meals to the homeless and downtrodden and then helping with the washing up.

Jake walked the walk.

His day job ironically was working in an advertising agency. Ironic because advertising was, more often than not, not the solution but the problem. It tried to get people to buy things they did not need and often could not afford. But Jake got around this ethical dilemma by creating advertising for the agency's pro-bono clients: the homeless shelter he volunteered at, the local food bank, and a no-kill animal shelter, to name a few. Because the agency made no money on these accounts, it could not afford to pay Jake a large salary, but Jake lived modestly, and he earned enough to pay the bills, plus, he did get benefits.

The agency also did political advertising and not always for the most honorable politicians. Recently the agency had signed a contract to do a reelection campaign for a most unsavory member of the House of Representatives, who stood for just about everything Jake despised. It made him cringe to think about it. The politician fancied himself a rogue cowboy and always wore a large Stetson hat. He went by the name and slogan: Clint Conroy, the Cowboy Congressman. Conservative and Proud of It. And he represented a district that had never in modern, or even ancient times, elected a Democrat. It was simply unheard of.

Clint Conroy went to church every Sunday with his wife, Lilly Mae, and their three girls, Faith, Hope, and Charity. While he maintained the image of the good church-going family man, it was no secret that Cowboy Clint was a bigot, a racist, a crook, a gambler, a bully, and a substance abuser who used his campaign funds to pay for his pleasures, which included a trio of women housed in upscale apartments — none of whom was named Faith, Hope, nor Charity — where he spent most of his time when he was in Washington, DC. He was on the payroll of almost every lobbyist on K Street. And as the joke went, these were just his good points.

But wait. It gets better. Clint Conroy cheated his two siblings out of their inheritance from their father, Connor Conroy, of the Conroy Capital Corporation, and then managed to squander most of this money on wine, women, and bad investments. He was perilously close to being bankrupt, both physically as well as morally.

...

As noted earlier, Jake had very high principles, and so everybody on the advertising account was stunned when Jake volunteered to work on The Cowboy Congressman's ad campaign. Jake was even a little amazed himself.

Congressman Conroy's opponent was a bright and charismatic Latina woman who had served several terms in the state Senate and was popular with the voters in her district. The timing was right for her to move up to the House of Representatives. She had been married for thirty-four years to a former Major League Baseball legend, and they had two grown children, one a veterinarian and the other a popular professor at the state university. If you were casting for a commercial for the All-American family, this was it.

...

Jake was fairly sure Congressman Conroy's younger opponent would not be basing her campaign on exposing Congressman's Conroy's dishonesty and lack of character, or on how the congressman had misused his campaign finances for his own personal use, or on exposing how Congressman Conroy's voting record had consistently favored the very wealthy and special interest groups and never the common man. Her campaign, he felt confident, would instead be full of hope. It would promise better health care, a higher minimum wage, a switch to renewable energy, and better education for all, including free college tuition for those who qualified. What Cowboy Conroy would refer to as "A liberal load of bull crap!"

Jake decided to take the bull by the horns and attack the congressman's opponent with insults, insinuations, and bold-faced lies. He would accuse his opponent of everything *he* was guilty of. When his opponent went high, The Cowboy would go low. The Cowboy would suggest that her first child was born suspiciously close to the time she was married and the real father was not her husband. That her family had come to the US illegally by crossing the border from Mexico, just like all the other criminal Mexicans who entered the US illegally to take jobs from the hard-working members of the congressman's district. That she and her husband ran a pedophile ring out of their basement. And finally, The Cowboy would wrap himself in the flag of the United States of America and declare himself the candidate who best represented real American values. Congressman Clint Conroy, The Cowboy, who will round up all those little doggies and send them all back to Mexico.

...

Congressman Conroy arrived at the ad agency with his

entourage and a very attractive young woman in tight jeans and dark sunglasses — his personal assistant, he announced with a wink — to review the campaign. They were ushered into the conference room and treated to beer and barbecue before they settled down to review the campaign.

The agency president — decked out in boots, a vest, and a ten-gallon hat — introduced Jake as the brilliant young man who had created a dynamite campaign that just might send The Cowboy all the way to the White House.

Jake asked for the lights to be dimmed and played the commercials on the agency wide-screen, high-definition TV. And what The Cowboy saw made him happy. Ecstatic, really. It was guaranteed to make every one of those damn liberals puke and fire up his base into a voting frenzy. The commercials were full of racial slurs, innuendo, bold-faced lies, and promise after extravagant promise that The Cowboy had no intention of keeping.

...

The reelection effort was going along better than expected, thanks in no small part to Jake's brilliant ad campaign. All the polls had Cowboy Clint Conroy up by double digits, and his reelection was a sure thing. It sure was. Or was it?

...

Jake had a good friend who specialized in a video-editing process called "deep fakes." Deep-fake videos are a dark process in which live footage of a real person can be made to say something entirely different but in the same exact voice. The result is a video that is totally convincing. And as it so happened, Jake's friend, like Jake, happened to be a liberal's liberal. Combining their talents, they produced a deep-fake version of the last commercial that was switched with the approved commercial just before the people went to the polls. They were confident the doctored commercial would be the end of Cowboy Conroy's career as a politician.

The night before the election, on social media and every TV station throughout the state, Cowboy Clint Conroy, Lilly Mae, and their three angelic girls, Faith, Hope, and Charity, appeared in a commercial in which, instead of hearing Cowboy Clint proclaim his love of God and love of country, millions heard the congressman tearfully admit to having run a pedophile ring out of his office, for which he would be ashamed the rest of his natural life. And no less egregious, Conroy admitted to having had relations with a neighbor's pet goat. For many years. Possibly a decade. All the while, Lilly Mae and the three girls smiled beatific smiles for all the world to see.

Meanwhile, a furious Congressman Conroy was swamped with phone calls, emails, tweets, and texts from around the state, around the country, and around the world with indignant demands for his resignation, for his imprisonment, for his life.

Jake, who was by now the target of a manhunt by his employer, was nowhere to be found. His apartment was vacant, and his landlord had no forwarding address. He had vanished off the face of the earth. His last words, his friend revealed were, "I don't wish ill of anyone, even those to whom I wish great ill!"

...

In spite of the last-minute bogus televised confession, Congressman Conroy still managed to win by a slim margin of 367 votes. Apparently his supporters would rather vote for a pedophile and a goat fornicator than vote for a Democrat. So in the congressman's mind, it was all's well that ends well. He won, fair and square. By a landslide!

...

The next morning, people around the state and around the country learned of the congressman's death after being shot and fatally wounded by his humiliated wife, Lilly Mae. He was rushed to the regional medical center, where he lived long enough to swear to the almighty God that he was innocent of all charges. And then he closed his eyes for the last time and passed on. Presumably downward, not upward.

Within one week, the advertising agency had lost all its accounts and the owners filed for Chapter 11.

And somewhere in the universe, the God of Karma thumbs through his book until he comes to Jake's entry, jots down, "Republican" under NEXT LIFE, and turns to the camera and winks.

A Walk
Down Memory Lane

WHEN I WAS FIFTEEN, I had a girlfriend who lived about five miles away from our house. My mom would drive me over to my girlfriend's house, and I would hang out, maybe have dinner, and watch a little TV with her mom and dad after dinner.

Her dad always offered to drive me home, and I always refused, saying that I didn't mind walking home, I needed the exercise. And the streets at night in our neighborhood were perfectly safe.

The offer having been made, my girlfriend's dad and mom would then excuse themselves and turn in.

And this is when the exercise of which I speak began. I was a teenage boy, and my hormones were raging.

After a few hours of making out and steaming up the windows, eventually, I had to say goodnight, and make good on my promise, and walk the five miles home.

...

About ten minutes into my journey home, I would pass

a house, a very large and impressive house on the right side of the road, where my mother, her brother and sister, and my grandparents had once lived. The house had been built in the 1930s and, at the bottom of a long driveway, had a distinctive mailbox that was a miniature replica of the grand old house itself.

My mother's family sold the house many years before I was born, but my mom used to tell me stories about the house and the wild parties they had there when my mom and her siblings were in college. So passing this house where my mom was raised always evoked a bit of nostalgia.

After I passed the house, I had a lot of time to weigh the merits of not accepting a ride home versus the opportunity to practice my moves on the couch. The couch always won. And walking home was not unpleasant.

...

When I turned sixteen, I got a summer job at a very posh department store in town, Sanderson's. I had been to this department store with my mother dozens of times when I was growing up to buy clothing for the next school year or to buy gifts for my mom, my dad, and my brother. The ceilings were high, and the lighting was amazingly soft and subtle. Everything was so fresh and clean. The glass countertops were always polished, and the merchandise was attractively displayed. It all looked just like a movie version of an upscale department store.

This was my first real job, and I made $1.25 an hour!

My first summer at Sanderson's, I worked as a stock boy in the Infants department. The salesladies were all my grandmother's age, as was the manager of the department. The salesladies fussed over and grandmothered me as if I were their own grandchild. Often they would insist on climbing up on a ladder in the stockroom to get something heavy down from a high shelf — because it was too dangerous for me!

The employees' part of the store, where I spent most of my time and which was behind the curtained exits, was not elegant like the "floor." It was darker, the ceilings were low, and instead of carpeting it had industrial linoleum.

I learned every item in the inventory, always showed up on time, and did my very best to earn my $1.25 an hour.

...

When I returned the following summer, the Infants department had a permanent stock boy, but the personnel manager asked me if I would like to work in sales. She said they had an opening in the Boys and Campus department.

And so I learned to use a cash register and to do a charge sale with a charge-a-plate (the forerunner of the credit card). I was instructed that no matter how old a lady was, you never called her Ma'am. It was always Miss. And other things like that. We were expected forty-five minutes before the store opened to make sure the glass counter tops were polished and all the merchandise on display was folded to perfection. We were not paid for this time however. Nor the thirty minutes after the store closed when we would turn in our sales receipts for the day and close out the cash register. But I was earning real money, and I had no complaints.

Being the same age as the young men the clothing was designed for was a plus. Moms frequently asked for my advice or had me try on a coat or sweater to see how it would look on their sons.

The top saleslady in our department was a grandmotherly type with bright eyes and an eager puppy-dog smile that reminded me of a Pomeranian. She could intuitively know which customer was going to make a big purchase as opposed to someone who was only there to window shop. When a customer came into the department, she would either race to get to the customer first, or she would pretend to be picking lint off of the sweaters. The customers that I was sure would buy out the department and give me the top sales for the day usually purchased a handkerchief or some boxer shorts, if anything at all. "Just looking," most would say.

One day though, I got lucky. The Pomeranian was on her break, and so she was not there when an attractive woman came into the department and it was my turn to assist.

Something immediately struck me about this woman. She was youngish, maybe in her mid-thirties, about five foot four, with red hair and pale blue eyes. Unbelievably, she looked *exactly* like photos of my mom that I had seen in her college yearbook. This woman could have been my mother from an earlier age. The resemblance was chilling.

I helped her pick out a full wardrobe of school clothes for her son who attended the grammar school across the street from the department store. She purchased enough clothing to give me the top sales for the day. I knew the Pomeranian would be pounding her head against the wall because she missed this one.

While most customers paid cash or wrote a personal check, this woman used a charge-a-plate to charge her purchase. The charge-a-plate was a rectangular metal object about one and a quarter inches by three inches and had the name and address of the holder in raised letters stamped onto it like a military dog tag. The charge-a-plate fit into a small device with a handle. The sales receipt and carbons were inserted into the device on top of the plate, and the handle pulled down to imprint the information on the receipt.

When I saw the address on the charge-a-plate, I was momentarily stunned. It was the very same address as the house with the mailbox that I walked past on my way home from my girlfriend's house. The very house my mother had grown up in!

I handed back the charge-a-plate and the receipt to the customer and asked her casually if the house at this address was the one with the mailbox that was a replica of the actual house.

She replied somewhat surprised, "Yes it is. Do you know the house?" And I casually answered, "I have walked past it a few times and was intrigued with the mailbox." To say more would probably have totally creeped her out. It really creeped me out.

...

I left my old neighborhood shortly after that summer and was away for almost a decade. I married after college and decided to remain in Bethesda, Maryland. But a few weeks ago, my wife and I visited the area to attend a wedding, and I was keen to show her where I had grown up. Of course I had to also show her the house with the mailbox where my mother grew up. While many homes on the street had changed immensely — some had hedges taller than the homes to protect their owner's privacy, others had been torn down and McMansions put up in their place — the family home had hardly changed from when I used to walk past it. It was virtually the same, including the mailbox that looked just like the house.

As we drove by the house, a young man, perhaps in his late teens, was walking down the long driveway, possibly to get the mail from the mailbox. I stopped the car and gawked. I think my wife could see it too. The young man, who was walking down the driveway from the house in which my mother and her siblings had grown up, looked exactly, exactly as I had in my first year of college. Right down to the part in his hair.

A Short Story

After forty-five years on this planet, I finally made the connection between the number of days in a calendar month and the number of days between full moons. It would not be incorrect to say I am not very observant.

Only recently, I made a discovery concerning highway construction workers. But unlike the moon/calendar connection, this discovery was not as obvious.

I was driving to my workplace in Albuquerque, New Mexico, USA – we New Mexicans always add the USA because an awful lot of people think that New Mexico is a foreign country. In fact, some businesses outside of New Mexico won't sell to people who live in New Mexico for the same reason: they don't ship outside the country. I blame this misconception on the people who present the weather on the TV news. The weatherman or weatherwoman always stands in front of New Mexico on the map of the country. And he or she points to the left and talks about the weather in Arizona and California. Or she or he points to the right and talks about the weather in Texas and the eastern part of the country. They never talk about New Mexico. They would have to step to one side if they were going to do that. And they never do.

Anyway . . . Aside from being somewhat slow on the uptake, I sometimes get distracted and veer off topic. I also have been accused of being "too literal."

Here's an example: my wife Mary Ellen and I were driving to Trader Joe's, that's where we do our shopping. Have you tried their turkey meatloaf? It's incredible. Anyway . . . We were driving to Trader Joe's — now where was I going with this? Oh right, we were driving to Trader Joe's and having a lively discussion. I had just pulled up alongside a red Chrysler that was stopped at the traffic light, and inside the car there were two couples waving their arms and talking in a very animated way. While we were at the stop light, my wife was continuing our conversation "Look at the Italians!" she said. I was taken aback. My wife is very smart, there is no doubt about that, but I asked, "How do you know they are Italians?" She looked at me and patiently explained, "I was talking about style, dear. About how some people dress."

"Oh," I said. "Those Italians."

See what I mean?

Now where was I? Oh, yes, I was driving to my place of employment in downtown Albuquerque. I work in advertising. I'm an account executive for a medium-size advertising and public relations company. Our office is on the tenth floor, and sometimes I take the stairs instead of the elevator for exercise.

Last year my company picked up the Albuquerque Parks and Recreation Department advertising account. The client doesn't have a very large budget, but we have been able to do some award-winning creative work for them.

Jack McKenzie – he was the creative group head on the account – came up with a brilliant billboard campaign. They were all over town. The billboards. Each board featured a beautiful photo of a different park. And each board had the headline **PARK IT HERE!** See what I mean? It was absolutely brilliant, and lots of people have commented on it. There was a story about the billboards in the *Albuquerque Journal*, and one in *ABQ*, our local city magazine. The campaign got a nice mention in *Advertising Age*. Our public relations department was responsible for placing the stories.

My favorite was the billboard for the Balloon Fiesta Park. Every October Albuquerque hosts the Balloon Fiesta, and we get hundreds of balloons in all shapes and sizes from all over the world. They have one day when all the balloons are shaped like giant cows, bottles of ketchup, Snoopy, pirates, and stuff like that. The billboard for the Balloon Fiesta Park featured a dramatic night photo of what they call "The Balloon Glow." One night during the fiesta, all at the same time, all the balloons fire up their heaters that produce the hot air inside the balloons and that make the balloons rise, and the flames from the heaters make all of the balloons glow like they are some kind of magical lights. It's a sight to behold. Don't miss it if you ever get the chance.

Jack's no longer at the agency, by the way: on the strength of the PARK IT HERE campaign, he was hired away by Mammoth & Bland. They're our main competitors. They occasionally do some pretty creative advertising. We're not too bad ourselves, but they do a better job of self-promoting, something we need to do more of.

Anyway . . . I was driving to work, and there was a construction project. The city of Albuquerque was widening the bridge that goes over the Rio Grande River and adding an additional lane in each direction. It was a huge project and frequently jammed up the traffic in both directions. These traffic delays went on and off for two years. It really was a mess.

You see, the Native Americans own large tracts of land in Albuquerque and throughout the state. So in many places there are no public roads that cross the pueblo land. That's the Native American land. So the traffic tends to concentrate on the few roads that actually get from one side of the river to the other and connect to the I-25, the freeway that runs in and out of Albuquerque and north and south, all up and down the state.

One day, the day I was talking about actually, because of the traffic tie-ups, it took me over two hours to go less than three miles. And needless to say, I was late for work. Very, very late.

I'm normally a punctual person. I would rather arrive thirty minutes early to an appointment than to be two minutes late. I think I have always been like this. Even as a child. I was always the first in all my classes to be in my seat and ready to absorb the lesson of the day. Even for math, which I was not that good at. I have a problem with those thought questions like "If John has 55 cents, and apples are three for 25 cents, and John wants to get a Snickers Bar that costs 5 cents, and a can of Pepsi that costs 15 cents . . . " and then they always ask something like "how many copies of *MAD Magazine* could John buy?" How the hell could anyone know that? Do you see what I mean?

My problem was I would look at the multiple choices, and if one matched the answer I came up with, I would pick that answer, which was usually wrong. There was one time I got the answer right. Though, as I remember, it was more of a lucky guess. You might call me math-challenged.

Anyway . . . While watching the construction workers with their fluorescent orange vests and their white hard hats – have you ever wondered why those hard hats always seem to sit higher on the head than they should? Why they don't come down over the ears? I think it might have something to do with the fact that they sit high on the head so if a steel beam falls on your head, the distance between the beam and your head will cushion the force. But don't quote me on this, I might be wrong. There is probably a more scientific answer.

OK. Here is what caught my attention, which you might have noticed does tend to carom about like a hockey puck. They all appeared to be the same height – the highway construction workers not the hockey puck. My guess – without having a tape measure – is they were all about five foot seven inches tall.

So maybe my observation was a fluke. It wouldn't be the first time. But then I began to notice that every time I drove through a road construction project – and I really do try to avoid driving through road construction projects if I can help it – it was the same. They all had the orange vests and the white sitting-too-high-on-their-heads hard hats, and they all appeared to be the same height, about five foot seven inches! Is that incredible or what? They are uniformly on the short side.

And then of course I could not help it: I started to sing that terrible song by Randy Newman, "Short People."

Short people got no reason

Short people got no reason

Short people got no reason to live

They got little hands

Little eyes

They walk around tellin' great big lies

They got little noses

And tiny little teeth

They wear platform shoes, on their nasty little feet . . .

I used to date a girl in high school who had very small feet. I used to kid her about avoiding strong winds. I told her she might blow over like a cardboard cutout. Not sure why, but we only went out one or two times.

And then of course – you know how my mind wanders

– I started remembering jokes, like someone once asked Danny DeVito, who is very short – did you know that? – if he (Danny) could loan him a dollar. And Danny replied, "I'd like to help you out pal, but I'm a little short!" Or maybe it was Marty Feldman.

Or, how do short people greet one another? They give each other a microwave. Or, I love this one: a tall person says I'm about six feet tall. A short person says I'm five feet, 4 point 75867 inches. Here's my all-time favorite: "How short am I? I'm so short I have to look up to see down!"

And remember, I was still stuck in this terrible traffic jam watching these identically short construction workers, and I thought about shortness of breath, or if you are short and skinny do you have shortness of breadth?

Of course I should have known this would be the day my cell phone died, and I had no way to let them know at the office I was trapped in the traffic nightmare from hell.

So to pass the time, I started making a mental list of all the things I could think of that had the word "short" in them, like: short circuit; short-sighted; a few cards short of a deck; short-order cook; short change; the long and the short of it; short list; short cut (boy, could I have used that then); short end of the stick (or if it were a height-challenged comedian, the short end of the shtick?); in the short term; boxer shorts (and short boxers); life is short; and of course, what you're reading here, a short story.

And all this time, most of these same-size, not-at-all-tall highway workers were standing around talking. Only a few of them ever did anything. Most of them just hung around in small groups talking. About what? How short they were?

I finally managed to get into the office. It was 10:57, and I had missed two meetings, including a creative presentation to the Albuquerque Parks and Recreation clients. This was the agency's first important presentation since Jack McKenzie jumped ship. The receptionist handed me a stack of phone messages for calls I had missed. It was a mess. And after running up ten flights of stairs, rather than wait for the elevator, I was, dare I say, a little short of breath.

When I got home that night, totally frazzled, I hung up my coat, and loosened my tie. I made myself a Martini; poured a glass of Chardonnay for my wife, Mary Ellen; sorted through the day's mail; patted Millie, our poodle; and waited until Mary Ellen asked me how my day was. I responded, "Do you want the long answer or the short answer?"

How I
Met My Wife

IT WAS A HOT, STEAMY NIGHT in Southern California. Electricity was in the air. There were uncharacteristic sounds of thunder in the distance: Los Angeles almost never had thunder storms. I was young, well, youngish. I had just turned thirty-two. I had been working in advertising as an art director at my first real advertising job. For five years I had been working on a Japanese car account. I thought I was pretty cool. I drove the awesome sports car our client manufactured, and I smoked little mini cigars. I had very hip boots with brass buckles on the side and square toes. I was somebody. Or at least I thought I was. More likely, I was a legend in my own mind. And I was about to go to the party to end all parties.

...

I got a late start in my advertising career. First I wasted two years in a junior college trying to figure out what I wanted to do when I grew up. Then I decided I wanted to go to art school and train to do something in the world of commercial art, but what that might be, I had no idea. So I spent the next four years at art school finding out. I gravitated toward advertising and graphic design. But in those days you had to be good at hand lettering to be a graphic designer, and I was not. But I liked designing ads, and I was pretty good with headlines and ad concepts. So advertising it was.

Just before I graduated, I received two really good offers from national ad agencies.

I had been at my first job six months, and everything was going great. And then I received my draft notice to report for my Army physical. This was in the late '60s, and we were fighting an undeclared war in Vietnam. I had used up my last deferment the minute I graduated.

In the six months I had been getting paid to do something that I loved doing, being an advertising art director at a major advertising agency, I had been eating and drinking a lot at lunch. My waistband had increased several inches. This was not cool. And so when I lined up in only my white Jockey briefs at the Army site for my physical, I felt rather old and portly standing in line with a bunch of very fit eighteen and nineteen year olds. But heft did not matter. The Army needed bodies, and if you were breathing, even barely, you were 1A. I *was* breathing. I was classified 1A. In three months' time, I was out of advertising and into Basic Training at Fort Ord in Monterey, California.

I spent my two years in uniform serving my country. It had its moments, but basically it was two more years of my life wasted. The best part, if I had to pick a best part, was I never got sent to Vietnam. I did maps for the Army Corp of Engineers and never left the Washington, DC, area. Because in my deplorable physical condition, which was only slightly improved after basic training, if I had been sent to Vietnam, I might not be writing this story about how I met my wife.

...

When I honorably parted ways with the U.S. Army, I was hired at my first real job, and this gets us back to where I started. The hot and humid night in Southern California. I bet you thought I had forgotten?

I was invited to a party by a lady art director from another advertising agency who I dated from time to time. She had been invited to the party by the company throwing the party, Stat's All There Is, a company that made Photostat copies of images that we used for layouts and print production. They made only Photostats, hence the name, Stat's All There Is.

I had not been invited by Stat's All There Is because at my agency we used a different Photostat company. But Stat's All There Is was famous for their parties and their food, and it was also a great place to hang out with other creative people from the business. No way had I wanted to miss this. So I accepted the invitation to be my lady art director's date.

...

The party was held behind the Stat's All There Is building in a large parking lot, and when we arrived, the party was in full swing. There was a live rock band, a bar, an endless table of catered food, and a ton of ad people, talking, eating, drinking, and dancing. Guys with long hair, many with beards, girls with long hair and short skirts.

At the time, I thought I was totally hip in my pin-stripe denim jacket and matching-pants leisure suit, my baby blue — to match my eyes — polyester, printed tie dye-patterned t-shirt, and my most excellent boots with the square toes. Looking back today, I might not have looked as cool as I thought I was. But, hey, what did I care? I was here. At the Stat's All There Is annual legendary bash.

...

No sooner had we entered the throng, than I spotted a young woman whom I knew only vaguely from art school who had married one of my classmates. I think her name was Nel or Nelly. And I think she had been a freshman at school when I was a senior. Anyway, Nel marched right up to me — my date had wandered off to say hi to some of her friends — and Nel said, "Duke!" like she and I were the best of friends. I would be astounded if we had ever said more than one or two words to one another. But there she was, and she said, "Duke, I want you to meet some of my friends." Duke! Nobody called me Duke. My name was Guy. Duke was a nickname someone gave me at art school as a joke, and it seemed to stick. My greatest fear in life is that at my funeral when some rent-a-rabbi is doing my service from the sparsest of notes, that this rabbi, whom I have never met, will refer to me as Duke! Oy! But I'll be dead, so I guess it won't really matter.

Ah, I remember now, her name was Melanie, but everyone called her Mel. Mel, Nel, I was close. Anyway, Mel introduced me to her friends, all of whom I believed were employed by Stat's All There Is. The third of these introductions was Marina. My eyes locked onto her and never left — even though I think there were three or four more introductions. I really don't remember. Marina was gorgeous. Beautiful, fresh, with long dark hair and bangs that came right down to her eyebrows. She was thin and had huge questioning eyes and a great figure, and she was wearing a really cool, red-patterned mini-skirt, and a British-racing-green colored tank top, plus a pair of really exotic crescent-shaped golden earrings. Her smile almost knocked me over. I was smitten.

Unfortunately, by this time, my date had shown up to claim ownership, and Marina went back to talking with Mel and her friends.

...

For the next several hours while dancing and schmoozing with people I knew at the party, my eyes were riveted on Marina, who seemed to be having a great time at the party. I had been long forgotten.

...

I was at the bar getting a couple of beers for me and my date when Mel appeared at my side, and she asked if I was having a good time. I cut to the chase and said, "I am totally in love with Marina. You have to introduce us again. I don't think she even noticed me," I added somewhat pathetically.

And that, I figured was that. I would have to somehow get Mel's phone number, and then call and ask for Marina's phone number, and then hope that she, Marina, remembered me. And in all likelihood, she probably wouldn't.

But then, out of the blue, Marina was standing before me. I think my date had wondered off again. Marina looked at me with those huge eyes and said, "Hi, you wanna dance?"

I was stunned. My heart was thumping in my chest. But I managed to casually toss off, "I thought you would never ask."

...

So on one of the hottest, most humid nights of the summer, with thunder booming in the distance, we danced to the live music. Our eyes locked onto one another's. Marina did this thing that some women do, looking from one eye to the other. I'm not even sure how to explain it, but it was very sexy. It was as if she was saying, "Go on I'm listening." I was a goner. I was going down with the ship.

The song went on forever, and I was starting to sweat.

After we exchanged names, I asked, "So, what do you

do?" expecting the answer to be she worked at one of the advertising agencies. She definitely looked like a creative type. Probably an art director with those incredible gold crescent earrings.

"I'm a stripper," she said, and then before I could interpret this the wrong way, she added, "A photographic stripper. I assemble many negatives into one master negative from which we make a composite photostat."

"Ah," I said, "That kind of stripper." And we both laughed as if this were the funniest thing we had ever heard. "How does one get to be a stripper, a photographic stripper, that is?" I asked.

"It's a long story," Marina said.

"Maybe you could tell me over dinner next week?" I responded, pleased with how smoothly I had asked her out, and terrified she would say no.

...

Our first date was almost perfect, in spite of the gaff I made while ordering for both of us; I asked Marina what kind of dressing she wanted on her Caesar Salad! Oh, and knocking over my glass of Mateus Rosé, which I had pronounced Mate-ious Rose. I guess if she was going to dine and dash, that would have been the ideal moment. But the evening went well, and we talked about everything under the sun, and then some. And as the evening went on, we stopped trying to impress each other, and we just had some good conversation while getting a picture of who each of us was.

...

After dating for several weeks and boring everybody at my office with my endless recounting in minute detail of our dates — what movie we saw, where we ate, what we ate, what we talked about — things seemed to be going well, and I asked Marina to come to my house for dinner. I was happy when she asked what time and what could she bring.

I lived alone with my cat, a tortoise shell cat that for reasons I don't remember was named Butternut. I think most likely it was because the fur on the left side of her hind leg was the color of butternut squash. As is true for any self-respecting cat in a creative household, she was known — by me at any rate — by many names, Squash, Squashy, The Nutztsker, Nutskya, Nutstoyoffsky or, sometimes, just The Cat.

I had been dating a lot of women before I met Marina, and the very second any of these women set foot inside my house, Butternut was out the cat door and remained outside until my visitor had left. So I was astonished when Butternut did not even look up when Marina came into the house. And after the obligatory tour, when Marina sat down in the living room on one of my canvas director chairs, Butternut jumped right onto her lap. She folded her paws in front of her, and started immediately to purr. I took this as an endorsement. "This one," Butternut seemed to be saying, "is a keeper."

"What a friendly kitty!" Marina said.

If you only knew, I said to myself. "Yes, isn't she though," I lied.

...

A few weeks later, and after a lovely visit in which Butternut and Marina were inseparable, and everything felt like it was really going great, I said somewhat on the spur of the moment, "Why don't you move in with us?"

I expected Marina would be happy. Maybe even ecstatic. But she looked sad, almost angry.

Now, I'm sorry, I neglected to mention, Marina and I had both been previously married. Both our marriages were short and best to have been gotten out of quickly. And as a footnote, this was in the 1970s, before Ruth Bader Ginsburg campaigned for legislation that would forever change women's lives for the better.

After a really awkward moment, Marina said, "After my divorce from Nicholas, I was asked to cut up my credit cards, in front of the attorney, even though I was the one who was working, not my husband. I had to have my ex-husband sign so I could get a phone and have the utilities in my apartment hooked up. I left the marriage with virtually nothing except my Volkswagen, my crescent earrings, and the shirt on my back. It took me a long time, but I managed to furnish the apartment myself on what I made working at Stat's All There Is. My bed, my refrigerator, my stereo record player, everything in that apartment is mine. I worked hard for all of it. I am not going to give all that up on the chance that this time things might work out!" And then she said, "I'm sorry, I have to go," and she left.

Wow! She might as well have hit me in the head with a two-by-four. I was stunned. But of course, the more I thought about it, the more I realized she was absolutely right. If things did not work out, I was OK. I had my house and everything in it. While Marina would have to start from scratch. It was unfair and unthinking for me to have made the invitation. Plus, as I only learned many years later, Marina's philosophy was TRUST NO ONE, and "no one" included me. We would just take it a day-at-a-time.

...

We continued to see each other — at first things were a little strained — but I would go to her place, or she would come to mine, and after a while we were back on more solid footing. Butternut, now Butternutter, still occupied Marina's lap every time Marina came to my house. And if only to the teeniest, tiniest degree, I think Marina began to trust me.

...

One night when I was at her apartment and we had just returned from a most excellent meal at Rosita's, the Mexican restaurant that was just around the block, Marina showed me the spare bedroom in her apartment that was always closed. In this room was a pile of beautiful pieces of honey-colored finished oak and a few metal wheels and other contraptions. I had no idea what I was looking at.

"What is all this?" I asked.

"It's a weaving loom," she said. "A friend of my ex-husband's and mine built it, and I tested his prototype. He eventually built a dozen and gave me this loom for being his test weaver. Only he and my ex-husband know how to put it together and how to take it apart. I never set it up here after the divorce because there is just not enough room."

And then Marina did something that brings tears to my eyes when I remember it today. She gave me one of the parts. She said, "Take this and put it in your spare bedroom. Each time I come to visit, I will bring another part. And if by the time all the parts are in your spare bedroom, and *if* we're still good, I will move in with you. If not," she said with a mischievous gleam in her eye and punching me in the arm, "you have to schlep all this back to my apartment. Deal?" she asked. "Deal," I eagerly agreed.

Over the following weeks and months, the pile of oak pieces at Marina's apartment grew smaller while the pile in my spare bedroom grew larger until finally, on a lovely spring day, with the enchanting smell of my blooming wisteria wafting on the air, Marina pulled up into my driveway in her much-loved Volkswagen and deposited the last piece of the loom in the spare bedroom. And on that weekend, we moved the rest of her belongings into *our* house. And the only individual who was happier than I was Butternutsy.

Nicolas, Marina's ex-husband — and actually a pretty OK guy it turned out — came to dinner one night and assembled the loom. I stood by in wonder at how each piece of oak fit perfectly into the next, until the loom was whole again, and Marina could take up weaving once more.

...

But, you're saying, the title of this story is "How I Met my Wife." So, when did you get married?

OK, here's the answer. Having been married before, neither of us was in any hurry to get married again. But one warm, sunny, bird-song-filled spring morning, just as Marina was getting into her Volkswagen, leaving for Stat's All There Is, I stopped her in the garage and said, "Roll down your window."

She rolled down her window, and I could tell she was impatient and worried she was going to be late to work, but what the hell. I got down on one knee, right next to the driver's-side window, and I said, "Will you marry me?" She laughed good-naturedly and said, "Guy, can we discuss this over dinner tonight?" We did, and she said, "Yes, of course. I thought you'd never ask!"

"But only on one condition," she said with her most faux serious grin, "That cheesy JC Penny 97-percent polyester, 3-percent cotton, tie dye T-shirt has to go to the Goodwill. This weekend, latest."

"Deal?" she asked. "Done deal!" I replied. One has to make some hard sacrifices for love, don't you know.

"Oh, and there's one more condition," she said pushing her luck. "If this does not work out, you have to promise to buy me a new bed, and refrigerator, and a new stereo. Not like the record player I had, but a new, state-of-the-art stereo, just like the one we have now." To which I agreed.

I'm happy to report, after forty-five years, things appear to be working out, but I don't want to get over confident. I have not had to buy her a new bed, refrigerator, or state-of-the-art stereo. And being married to Marina for the past forty-five years has been the single, easiest thing I have ever done in my life. If you're not familiar with the Yiddish word, *beshert*, look it up. It will explain everything.

In *the* Dog House

THERE'S AN EXPRESSION in the advertising business; "What have you done for me lately?" What it means is that even if you have won ten Gold Lions for creative excellence since you joined the agency, if you have not hit one out of the ballpark recently, you're chopped liver. Block that metaphor!

It's a vicious business. It really is. Being a creative person in advertising — an art director or copywriter — is a very competitive job. You are constantly competing against the other creative teams — quite often your best friends — to see whose campaign will win out over the others. In short, its dog eat dog. Sorry, there I go again.

Having the winning ad campaign is euphoric. Having the campaign that did not win sucks. And then, of course, the campaign has to be presented to the client, who may shoot it down, and then you're back to square one.

Let me give you an example. If you are old enough to remember the first VW campaign, this is what I am talking about. The agency that had the Volkswagen account did not try to compete with the longer, lower, sexier, all-new

1960s automobiles being produced by the Big Three Detroit automakers. It focused on what made the Volkswagen unique, which was its size. **Think Small** was the headline on the magazine ads, and on billboards all over town, and all over the country. More brilliantly clever ads with catchy headlines that emphasized the small car's advantages with just the right amount of well-crafted persuasive copy followed. The campaign got noticed, and what people initially perceived as a small, cramped, underpowered, and unsophisticated automobile, changed into a hip, fun, and economical alternative. A classic case of turning a lemon into lemonade.

The creative teams on the Volkswagen account probably created dozens of campaigns, each very creative in its own way. And yet, there was only one winner. The other teams might very well have been feeling the "What have you done for me lately" heat. See what I mean?

...

I had done pretty well at my previous agency and had won my share of creative recognition. But the politics at the agency — what one of my colleagues referred to as a nest of vipers, and he was being generous — was really getting to me. I felt like I had done more for them lately, much more, than they had done for me. It was time to move on.

So I did what every creative person does. I put together my portfolio of the ads and TV commercials I had created at the agency and my previous two agencies, and I called a headhunter. I got several interviews, and on the strength of my creative work, I got a senior-level position at one of the big multinational advertising agencies. (And the headhunter made another payment on her condo in Aspen.)

...

But the move turned out to be, to use another cliché, out of the frying pan and into the fire. The creative director who hired me thought my creative work was a good fit for the agency. But then he had probably been to the same headhunter I had been to (everyone in town used her) and he left the agency after my first month. He was replaced by an ostentatious, snobby creative director from London who wore bold quarter-inch striped shirts, smart silk ties, and bespoke suits from Saville Row.

Nigel, the new creative director, had meetings once a week showcasing all the really cutting-edge creative work that was coming out of London. He frequently encouraged us to do something "just like" [insert the current ad]. At one point I spoke up and said, "But Nigel, if we do ads just like another agency, aren't we going to get the reputation for being the agency that is just like the other agency?" Nigel's icy stare and forced laugh told me I would have been better off keeping that thought to myself. Smoke was coming out of the bullet holes in my foot.

Before Nigel came on board, I had been working on an ad campaign for an old and established Napa Valley winery. I'm sure we have all had a bottle of their finest when dining out on that special occasion. The client was very pleased with the ads that ran in some very upscale magazines. And I was pretty pleased with the campaign myself. But Nigel thought the ads were a "dog's breakfast" and said he was embarrassed for the client and embarrassed for the agency. And where, he wanted to know, did I find that photographer? "Wine is simply never photographed like that!" I was off to a rocky start. I could not help thinking, once again, I might have been better off staying in that nest of vipers.

In time, however, I redeemed myself in Nigel's eyes and did not have any more embarrassments, such as the winery ads or the snarky comment about the agency that is just like that other agency. But Nigel had not hired me, and every day I felt more and more like a hog on a sofa. I did my best to keep a low profile.

...

One blustery winter's day, I came to work in a wool fisherman's knit sweater over a thick Oxford-cloth shirt. I tend to run cold, and the agency had turned the thermostat down to save energy. It was a meat locker in there!

I had arrived at work early, as was my habit, and was enjoying a cup of coffee and a Cheese Danish and going through my mail from the previous day. I had my own coffee maker and bean grinder and always enjoyed two or three cups of real coffee, not the bilge water they had in the coffee room. And I *never* offered coffee to my co-workers even though they offered to pay. It was MY COFFEE. The room was chilly, and I was glad for my warm sweater. I put some cool jazz on my personal stereo and sat at my drawing board thinking about what I could do for my clients and the agency today.

There was a knock on my door and in walked Nigel! Of course he was looking like he had just stepped out of *Gentleman's Quarterly*. The London edition. Blue pin-striped suit, paisley silk tie and matching handkerchief, navy blue dress shirt, Berluti Italian shoes that must have cost more than I made in a week. The works. And there I sat in my faded Levis, my well-worn Nike trainers, and my white fisherman's knit sweater.

My first thought, and my second, and third thoughts were, "Here goes, I'm going to be fired. My work isn't British enough. He could hire two junior art directors for what the agency is paying me." As I think I said, Nigel had not hired me. I had no right occupying this large four-window office. And finally, "What had I done for him lately?"

I obsequiously offered Nigel a cup of my coffee. He accepted, and I bought myself at least another few minutes of employment. It was a major sacrifice given that I NEVER SHARE MY COFFEE.

My face flushed, and I started to sweat. My appropriately named sweater, which normally provided only a modicum of warmth, had become a sauna. I was sweating. Buckets. Buckets. And more buckets. Nigel could see the effect he was having on me and, even for a pretentious Englishman, I think he must have felt bad.

...

As casually as possible, I pulled the sweater off and set it on the back of my chair. I nonchalantly mopped back my soaked hair and made a futile effort to appear calm and composed. But I continued to sweat. I made a lame comment about how they needed to turn down the thermostat.

Nigel, who may well have been more embarrassed than I was as he watched me shed pounds of liquid, and who was probably thinking to himself, "Let no good deed go unpunished," announced that I was being promoted with a nice advance in pay. The agency, it would seem, was happy with what I had done for it lately. He congratulated me and escaped from my office probably thinking I was some kind of nut job!

And I went looking for a towel.

Looking Back

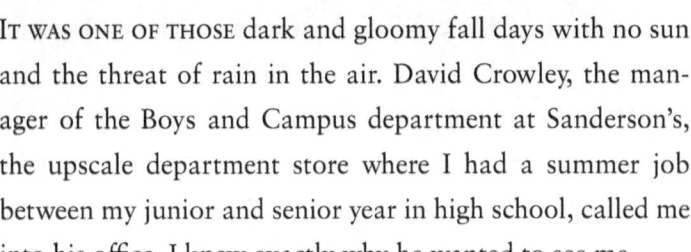

It was one of those dark and gloomy fall days with no sun and the threat of rain in the air. David Crowley, the manager of the Boys and Campus department at Sanderson's, the upscale department store where I had a summer job between my junior and senior year in high school, called me into his office. I knew exactly why he wanted to see me.

David Crowley came from a family in Grosse Pointe, Michigan, that owned one of the bigger department stores in that area. I have no idea why, but instead of working for the family business, he moved out west and took a job as a department manager.

Mr. Crowley was a very decent boss and, unlike some department managers I had worked for in previous summers at Sanderson's, he actually cared about his employees. Even those like me, who were only there for the summer.

I was hired as a junior salesman in the Boys and Campus department. It was a good job for a young high-school student because I was the age for which most of our merchandise was designed. And I liked to think that I was good at my job. Because of my age, I was asked for advice by a lot of the moms who were shopping for clothing for their sons. Plus, I got to wear sports jackets, slacks, and ties from the current inventory. And so I was always well dressed, and I also acted as a model for the merchandise.

...

Alan Birch, our assistant manager, was ten years younger than David Crowley and a spitting image of Paul Newman. Alan Birch had a wicked sense of humor. He and I got on famously. Possibly a little too famously.

Alan was not the best influence on me, I'm afraid to say. He was into practical jokes. For example, one time he telephoned one of the attractive young salesladies in the Lingerie department and asked if she had Ooh Làa Làa bikini panties, a line of very sexy French underwear. When the saleslady answered, "Yes, I have," which was department store speak for "Yes, we carry that line," Alan inquired, "Are you wearing them now?"

From where Alan was phoning, he and I could see the young lady blush, and when she looked up, Alan held up the phone so she could see it was he who had called, and he waved. Today that would be considered sexual harassment and grounds for instant dismissal, but back then things were not as strict. Alan encouraged me to do dumb things like that. And dumb things like that I did because I wanted to be just like him.

...

We had a grandmotherly saleslady in our department who had worked for Sanderson's for twenty years. Maybe longer. Her name was Mrs. Pomeroy. She was a smallish woman with large, moist eyes and an ingratiating smile, all of which reminded me of a Pomeranian dog. She always seemed ready to please. Alan Birch and I had many laughs over lunch in the cafeteria about "Mrs. Pomeranian," as we called her.

Mrs. Pomeroy was the top salesperson in the department, usually bringing in two-to-three hundred dollars in sales per day, which at that time was a lot. Moms and dads trusted her. I do not believe she had ever been married; the "Mrs.'" was more of an honorary title for salesladies of a certain age.

But there was a sly and cunning side to Mrs. Pomeroy that most people did not see. She had a kind of built-in radar and could spot someone who was going to spend a lot of money versus someone who was, "Just looking, thank you." If a customer came into the department who *was* just window shopping, Mrs. Pomeroy would pass this customer on to me saying that it was time for her break and would I be so kind as to assist?

On the other hand, if someone came into the department prepared to spend a small fortune, even if it was not her turn to assist, Mrs. Pomeroy was there and postured to please. Sometimes when I was waiting on a customer who surprisingly turned out to be a serious shopper, Mrs. Pomeroy would magically appear next to me and pull out merchandise from the drawer or the case that the customer would almost always add to his or her order. And then towards the end of the sale, Mrs. Pomeroy would ask me if I could help a customer who had just entered the department, and who was undoubtedly shopping for a handkerchief, or a tie, or something from the sale table, and she would write up *my* sale herself.

...

Over lunch in the cafeteria one wonderful crisp autumn day, it was just after a storm had passed, and the sky was that heartbreakingly brilliant shade of blue, Alan Birch and I hatched a most devious plot.

We would make a list of items from all over the department, then we would call Mrs. Pomeroy from a phone outside the department, pretend to be a customer, and watch her assemble the order from our list. Alan Birch encouraged me to make the call.

I told Mrs. Pomeroy, when she returned from her morning break, that a Mr. Harvey Smithson had called and wanted to order some clothing for his son who was about to return to school. He said he would call back when she had returned to the department.

Mrs. Pomeroy smiled and acted like she knew Mr. Smithson well. She went so far as to assure me that she had been serving Harvey Smithson and his son for many years.

...

That afternoon, instead of going to the cafeteria for lunch, I went to the department next to ours and called Mrs. Pomeroy. When she came to the phone, I disguised my voice and identified myself as Harvey Smithson. I said because we didn't have a lot of time, I needed her to set some things aside for Harvey Junior. Harvey Senior would bring Harvey Junior in to try on some things later that day. It took my entire lunch break, surreptitiously watching Mrs. Pomeroy retrieve the items on the list.

...

When I returned from my lunch break, Mrs. Pomeroy was standing proudly by a large pile of clothing that she had assembled from my list. She said in a proprietary tone, "My good friend Harvey Smithson called. He's coming in later today with his son, and he asked me to set some things aside." One or two things, she added, would have to be sent over from one of our other stores. I knew this of course because I had also called around for some items that were out of stock in our store.

I looked disappointed and said, "Gosh, Mrs. Pomeroy, that's a whole week's worth of sales for me. How do you do it? You *always* get the big sales!"

Mrs. Pomeroy looked me right in the eye and, with a straight face, told me that she had been waiting on Mr. Harvey Smithson and Harvey Junior for many years and that he was one of her "personal customers." She continued the fiction by filling in intimate details as she went along.

I waited for a few beats after she finished, and then I announced in the same voice I had used on the phone, "Mrs. Pomeroy, I *am* Harvey Smithson!"

Alan Birch and I had alerted all the other salespeople to the prank, and there was laughter all around. Mrs. Pomeroy did not look so cocky now. She looked embarrassed, then angry, and then sad.

...

David Crowley, our department manager, asked me to come into his office, to shut the door, and to have a seat. He said, "I think you know why you are here." He was smiling and said he had heard from Mrs. Pomeroy, no less, of my little practical joke.

Then he said that, yes, Mrs. Pomeroy could be a little much sometimes, and he admitted he was somewhat amused at my prank. But, he continued, whereas I would be leaving soon to return to my last year in high school and then off to college after that, Mrs. Pomeroy would be working in his department — he hoped — for many years to come. He reminded me that she was his top salesperson who generated the lion's share of profit for the Boys and Campus department. But, beyond all that, he continued, there was a fact she told very few people: she was also the caretaker of her elderly mother, who had come to the US from Manchester, England, and was housebound with dementia. Almost all of Mrs. Pomeroy's income went to the care of her mother. Her mother was a widow who had no particular skills, who had worked hard her whole life cleaning houses, taking in sewing and ironing, washing dishes in restaurants, any job she could get, so that she could put her daughter through school to give her only child, Mrs. Annette Pomeroy, a better life here in America.

I felt terrible. Not because what I did might have humiliated Mrs. Pomeroy, but because the incident made me look bad in the eyes of Mr. Crowley, who was very decent about my dumb trick.

Mr. Crowley said, "You are going to do three things: you are going to apologize to Mrs. Pomeroy in front of the entire department, you are going to cancel all the "sends" from the other stores, and you *will* return all the merchandise to stock. Right now."

...

All this happened when I was a brash young man with dark brown hair whose entire world was ahead of him. But as I write this, the brash young man is pushing seventy, and what hair he has left has been white for decades. What was hysterically funny then seems cruel and mean-spirited now.

I am sad that Mrs. Pomeroy is no longer with us, but if she were, the man with the thinning white hair would like to apologize in earnest and ask her forgiveness for the thoughtless trick he played on her so many years ago.

Because looking back with the eyes and the wisdom of age, what I thought was cute, and clever, and funny, was in fact stupid and immature. And I would hope that Alan Birch, wherever he is now, would join me in apologizing.

And for Mrs. Pomeroy, wherever you are, I wish you the best and brightest day ever. One of those cool, crisp autumn days, just after a storm has passed, and the skies are that heart-breakingly brilliant shade of blue.

Death

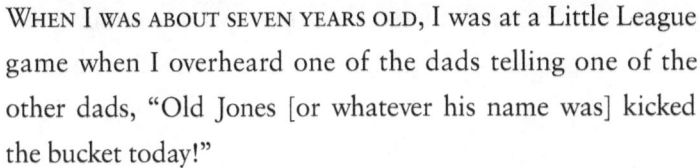

WHEN I WAS ABOUT SEVEN YEARS OLD, I was at a Little League game when I overheard one of the dads telling one of the other dads, "Old Jones [or whatever his name was] kicked the bucket today!"

It was the first time I had heard that expression, and so I went around telling my friends, "Old Jones kicked the bucket today!" We all laughed without having a clue as to why we were laughing or why someone would kick buckets.

When I got home, I casually told my mom, "Old Jones kicked the bucket today!"

Mom looked at me kind of funny, so I asked, "What does that mean? Old Jones kicked the bucket?" And she told me that it meant Old Jones, whoever he was, had died. "It's a slang expression, hon, for when someone dies. They say he kicked the bucket."

"Ah, I see," I said, though I really didn't.

And being a seven year old, I really had no idea about the concept of dying or death.

"What happens when you die?" I asked.

My mother paused for a moment to think this through. "Well, some people believe that when someone dies and the life passes out of their body, their spirit goes up to heaven where it lives forever with all the other spirits of people who have died."

This explanation made no sense to me whatsoever.

My mom continued. "We don't believe in heaven, so when someone dies, it means that for one reason or another, the person who has died stops breathing, and his heart stops beating, his brain stops thinking. His eyes see nothing, his nose smells nothing. It's like when your watch stops running, except winding the watch will not make it run again." Back then people still wore watches that had to be wound every day. I got that bit.

I was doing my best to wrap my seven-year-old brain around this concept.

My mom continued, "When someone dies, his family and friends gather together and have a ceremony to remember him at a church or a synagogue. And then the person who has died is buried in the ground in a cemetery."

Now this explanation was really creeping me out. The thought of being buried in the ground was too much, and my small brain overloaded. I decided this was more than I really wanted to know. And I did not know it at the time, but I was so glad my mom did not get into cremation! Being buried in the ground was bad enough.

"Can we have hot dogs for dinner?" I asked. And mom gave me a big hug and said, "Sure, and I can make potato salad with sweet pickle relish if you want?" And that was the end of that.

...

I witnessed my first real dead person when I was eight and a half. I was walking home from school, and along the route was a building with doctors's offices. There was an ambulance in front, and the rear doors of the ambulance were open. As I approached, I saw two men in white uniforms wheeling out a gurney with a man who was lying on his back. His face was pale white, and there were blue veins showing on his face and neck. His eyes were closed. He was not moving, and I was pretty sure he was dead. The two ambulance men, when they noticed me standing there gawking, hastily covered the man's face.

When I got home, I told my mom what I had seen, and she said it definitely sounded like the man I saw on the gurney was dead. Wow, I thought, wait until I go to school tomorrow. I can tell all my buddies I saw a genuine dead guy who had obviously kicked the bucket.

...

When I was ten, Buggsy, our old Beagle, was sick and we had to take him to the vet where the doctor put him "to sleep." Buggsy had been sleeping most of the time anyway so this did not seem so final. "When will he wake up, I asked?"

But my mom explained that Buggsy Beagle had died. "Putting Buggsy to sleep, is just another way of saying, Buggsy

Beagle has died."

"Did Buggsy kick the bucket?" I asked.

"Yes, dear," mom replied. "Buggsy Beagle has gone to the great dog house in the sky where he can play with all the other dogs for eternity or maybe even longer. Which would be great if we believed that, but I'm afraid we don't, honey."

...

OK. I was ten now and I knew a lot more about life than I did when I was seven. But still this concept was very confusing. Dog houses in the sky? And now I was forced to ask my mom, "How long is eternity? A year? Ten years? A hundred years?"

Mom realized how literal my small mind was and said, "Eternity is forever. Eternity never ends. It just goes on and on and on and...."

"Ah, OK," I said. "But if eternity never ends, then when did it start?" I was treading heavily on one of the great imponderables here without even knowing it.

I think Mom knew she was in way over her head, and so she skirted the issue and said, "Do you want to go to Jenner's and get a hamburger and a malt?"

...

I managed to get by the next five years without having to deal with death. Of course hundreds of millions of people died, but not in my family. And then . . . .

My grandmother, who came to this country from the old country, Lithuania, was getting up there in years – my mom had been an "oops" who came along late in my grandmother's life – and grandma had been in poor health for as long as I could remember. She got pneumonia, and after a week in the hospital, she died.

I was really sad because even though she was a bit loopy, she was kind and generous and always referred to me as a genius. (The definition of a genius is a boy — or girl — with a Jewish grandmother.) Every year on my birthday, she gave me a crisp twenty dollar bill. And on mom's birthday, I got a bonus, a five dollar bill. And she loved to take me to Jenner's, the malt shop in town, where I could get my favorites: a hamburger with French fries and a butterscotch sundae with nuts, and whipped cream, with a maraschino cherry on top.

By this time, I was almost old enough to drive, and I was a lot clearer on the concept of death. But it still seemed confusing. When mom and I visited grandma in the hospital, she did not look great, but she was able to talk, and she and mom had a long conversation until the nurse came in and said we needed to leave. So the last time I had seen her, just a few days before in the hospital, she was alive, and then she wasn't. She was dead. She kicked the bucket, I guess.

How does this happen? One moment you're alive, and the next moment you are not. One moment you are breathing, your eyes are moving and seeing things, your lips are moving, and you are speaking. And the next moment, nothing.

I cried a lot. I missed grandma. And I asked my mother, "Where is grandma now?"

I knew we didn't believe in heaven or hell. Those are Christian beliefs, but grandma had to be somewhere. Mom said, and this was so great, "Grandma's physical self is gone, but her memory will be a blessing in our hearts forever. And every year on the anniversary of her death, we will light a candle and remember her and all that she meant to us." That's called a *yahrzeit* and is an old Jewish tradition.

To cheer us up, mom took me to Jenner's and I got my butterscotch sundae and mom got a bowl of chocolate cherry ice cream.

...

When I was twenty-five and living on my own, my dad died. My parents were divorced, but I tried to see my dad at least once every week or so. He died at home while playing his Hammond organ. My stepmom, Helen, called and said that he had been playing the organ and singing one of his favorite songs – I believe she said "I'll Be Seeing You" – when he lurched forward and died instantly from a massive heart attack. Helen was devastated, and so was I. Mom was sad too when I called to give her the news, even though she and my dad had been divorced for over twenty years. "He *was* your dad," she said, "and a very decent person. It's just we could never get along, and we fought about everything. And, oh, yes, he cheated on me almost from the day we were married. And he got fired from every job I ever lined up for him. But other than that . . . ."

After the funeral, I called mom and asked her to meet me at Jenner's, and we had the usual — my butterscotch sundae and her bowl of chocolate cherry ice cream. And we laughed in a humor noir sort of way about "old dad" having kicked the bucket. "Or at least the piano keys," Mom said, "It would be just like your dad to have struck a minor note with his nose." "Not nice," I said, as I ate the last delicious bite of my butterscotch sundae.

...

I was twenty-five then, working in advertising as an art director creating ads for products that nobody needed. But the pay was good and, as we liked to say, there was no heavy lifting. I was dating several women, but no one that I was close enough to, to want to settle down with and maybe have kids.

One of the partners at the agency I worked for had a terrible stroke and died within the week. I never had much to do with Ted, but he was a nice-enough guy, and I felt bad for his wife and his kids. He wasn't more than fifty-five. For once in my life I managed to hold my thoughts to myself and not joke that old Ted kicked the bucket. I would like to think I was maturing, but there was no way that was going to happen. My tongue was just sore from my biting it.

...

By the time I was thirty-two, I had met a terrific woman,

Marina, who was everything I had ever dreamed of and more. We met at an advertising party, and I knew immediately that this was the one. My cat, who never liked any of the women I dated, took to her immediately. She — Marina, not the cat — worked in the business too as a copywriter, so we were a pretty creative family. And like myself, Marina was an only child. We lived together for a few years and, when it looked like everything was working, we got married in Las Vegas in a very simple ceremony with only one friend, who was our witness.

Mom adored Marina, and Marina adored my mom. And you know, finding a woman who your mother approves of and who your cat loves is something of a miracle.

I would sit quietly while my mom exposed all my deep, dark childhood secrets. Occasionally I would groan, "MOM?" but it did no good. She really enjoyed sharing all the stories of my young years.

And, of course, it was only a matter of time before mom told Marina all about my discovering death at a tender young age. Naturally, kicking the bucket was a big part of this story.

But there was a fondness and tenderness to all these revelations, and perhaps it gave Marina some insights into who it was she had married.

...

Marina's mom had died at a very young age, forty-six, I think Marina said. Marina's mom was so young, and losing her mom when Marina was right out of college was something she never really got over. I only wish I had gotten to meet and know Marina's mom. She sounded like a really terrific person with a great sense of humor. I would have enjoyed hearing *her* stories about my wife when she was very young.

...

My mom was only fifty-six at this time, but already she had lived ten years longer than Marina's mom. My mom loved to play tennis and was in really great shape for her age. She was competitive, and she was good. She played in tournaments and won her fair share. Her mantel at home was covered with trophies.

So when she told Marina and me over lunch that she had inoperable cancer, we just could not believe it. She said that she was in great shape and that she was going to "beat this thing, 40 love, and in straight sets," was how she put it.

She didn't beat it. But she did not go down without a fight. And what a toll on her it took. In the end, I think hospice care would have been a better choice and would have provided a more dignified and peaceful way to die, rather than all the radiation and chemotherapy.

...

Marina and I have been married now for forty-seven years. We ask ourselves frequently how this can be true. We were so young when we married, and now we're in our seventies, and I am pushing eighty. We're on cats number seven and eight, and they are in their older years as well.

Many of our friends and several family members have died during these forty-five years. Numerous old friends from college, several aunts and uncles, and two of my cousins. But as I get older and closer to the end, kicking the bucket is not an expression I use any more. The novelty and sick humor of that expression is no longer amusing.

And yet, here we are. Everything is great. I can honestly say that I have never felt in better shape than I do as I write this story in my seventy-seventh year. Marina is just as pretty as the day we met at the advertising party, and I thank my lucky stars that I met such an incredible person who has been my life's companion for over half of my life. If I had to do it all over, there is not a single thing I would do differently.

We've lived in the same house with a wonderful view for over twenty years. We have many close friends in the community. We have both remained active and continue to create. I have had much success with my watercolor paintings of our beautiful mesas and mountains, selling most of my paintings at my gallery in Santa Fe, and I have a waiting list of commissions.

Marina has taken up weaving again, something she did before we met, and has built a tremendous reputation for her inventive use of color and intricate patterns. Her weaving flies off the loom and out the door as fast as she weaves it.

Every day, I wake up and thank the heavens for all the

wonderful things we have, for our good health, our good friends, our lovely house, and our fantastic little community of Gamble Oaks nestled in the foothills in the northern escarpment of the Sandia Mountain range. I don't think there is one thing we are lacking.

...

News article from *The Gamble Oaks Gazette:*

Gerald "Guy" Phister, a longtime resident of Gamble Oaks and husband of weaver, Marina Jones-Phister, died last night from injuries sustained in a fall. Phister, known for his watercolor landscape paintings was seventy-nine, thirty-seven days shy of his eightieth birthday. Marina Jones-Phister told the *Gazette* that her husband had gotten up around 2 AM to investigate a noise in the garage when he kicked and then stumbled over a bucket of paint that he had left out the day before for some touching up that he was planning to do to the front of their casita the following day. Phister hit his head on a shelf and was dead by the time the paramedics arrived.

From Marketing
to Marketing

Ted retired from advertising when he turned sixty-five. Medicare and Social Security were about to kick in, and he and Margie, his wife of thirty-nine years, wanted some time to travel and do the things they wanted to do before they were "too old." The kids were spread out across the country, and Ted and Margie felt it would be great to visit each of their children and get to know their grandkids before they were grown up.

Ted wanted to take up jogging again and to have lunches to "catch up" with his friends, most of whom were now also retired. He might even put on his tool belt and see to making some of those home repairs he had been putting off for "when he had more time."

And for the first few years life was good.

Except the kids were kind of cranky — though they did their best to hide it — about having to straighten everything up each time grandma and grandpa came to visit, and the visits were always a little too long and a bit like the proverbial three-day old fish. Besides, with Facebook, Ted and

Margie could follow the lives of their children, celebrate their achievements, and watch their grandchildren grow through the almost daily posting of photos without really having to travel.

International travel did not pan out either. The trips by plane that used to be so comfortable with decent snacks and meals became an ordeal. The seats were smaller, and there was never enough room for Ted's knees. Getting out of the seat to use the toilet was a chore, and then there was usually a wait when Ted's kidneys could not wait. The meals had become a choice of salted peanuts or five stale miniscule pretzels, even on the long flights.

Once they got to their destination, there were mobs of tourists, who were rude and pushy and expected Ted and Margie to speak their language! The hotels were expensive; and the amenities few; and the service, when you could get any, not ideal. The sights to be seen were so crowded with tours, tour buses, and tour guides speaking in foreign languages through bullhorns . . . what was the point?

Ted found that jogging at his age was a lot harder than it had been when he took it up in his thirties. And it was easier to call Jason, their local handyman, to do the home repair things, rather than Ted doing them himself. Jason was much better and tidier than Ted was. Jason actually finished what he started. And he charged so little for his time.

As for Ted's retired friends, all they ever wanted to do was reminisce about their younger days or complain about the way the country was being allowed to go to hell in a handbasket. Or talk about how much better and more efficient things were when *they* were working.

Margie, who had raised three children, had already established routines: having lunch with her girlfriends; attending her book club get-togethers; and going to the garden club meetings, her monthly Mahjong group, and all the other activities that had filled her days for most of the years when Ted was at work. During those years, she taught herself French, she read books, she learned to garden, and while the kids were at school, she attended painting and drawing classes at the local community college. She was what the human resources person at Ted's old company would have called a self-starter.

Ted, on the other hand, needed something to fill his days. Staring mindlessly at his laptop for hours on end following friends (many of whom he had never met and had not the least desire to meet) on Facebook, or obsessing over *The New York Times*, *The London Business Review*, The Motley Fool, and on and on online, for hours at a time. It was nothing more than a giant time suck.

He volunteered to do the laundry, go to the market, run the vacuum around, do the dishes, and take on other homey chores, just to have something to fill the hours between breakfast and dinner. He said he owed it to the marriage now that he was retired. It was payback for everything Marge had done while raising the kids while Ted was working.

...

At the local supermarket where he was becoming a regular, Ted was getting to know the checkers and some of the baggers. One of his talents as an account executive at the ad agency had been learning the names and family histories of clients and the people he worked with. Before he knew it, he realized he had learned a lot about each of the supermarket employees.

While he would be checking out he would make small talk with the checkers. "Hi, Brenda," he would say if Brenda was his checker. "How's Bob getting on after the hip replacement?" Or "Hi, Dave. How's Dave Junior's Little League going?" He knew a little something about everyone. He was a good listener, and he retained most of what he learned. He liked to say, "Just listen, and most people will tell you their life story."

...

One day when he came into the market, he realized that Helen Davis, one of his favorite checkers, had not been in for the last two or three times he had done his shopping. He asked Mary Beth if Helen Davis was OK. He'd not seen her recently. Was everything all right?

Mary Beth told Ted that Helen Davis and her family had moved to Wyoming. Her husband had gotten a good job offer, and the schools there were really excellent. Not to mention the blue, cloud-filled skies and clean air.

Mary Beth told Ted that they needed someone part time to work as a checker, until they could hire a permanent replacement. Did he know anybody?

"How about me?" Ted asked.

Mary Beth laughed. "Oh, sure, Mr. Advertising Executive working as a checker. That's a good one!"

But Ted was serious. "I need something to do with my time," he said. "Being retired is the most boring job I have ever had in my life. Do you think they would take me on?"

...

And so Ted Mathews, aged sixty-seven, embarked on a new career: checker at the Golden Egg Market & Deli on State Route 55. He mused that he had gone from "a career in marketing to a career in marketing." He was a fast learner and quickly learned how to scan the items with bar codes. He learned how to identify produce and what was today's price per pound. He learned how to scan coupons, how to process a credit card payment, and how to accept an iPhone ApplePay or other smartphone purchase. What he did not know was exactly how much a checker had to know, besides just ringing up purchases.

One thing he did not need to learn was how to chat up the customers, how to make them feel welcome, how to ask if they found everything OK or not OK.

Ted would ask customers if they liked a specific item in their cart. If the customer had a wine Ted had tried, he would say, "My wife and I had a bottle of this just last week; it's really excellent, isn't it?' Or "Those sweet potato fries are so tasty." He preferred his fries with lots of ketchup. He was a natural.

...

He got on well with the box boys and box girls who did the bagging. One of the baggers had been with the Golden Egg for eighteen years. He was slow. He probably had a mild intellectual disability, but he was a really conscientious bagger. He never missed a day of work, and he was sunny, and polite, and very efficient, and professional. He would put a rubber band around the plastic self-serve containers so the containers would not leak on the trip home. He put all the cold things in one bag, so the customer could put them in a cold case during hot weather. He had his techniques, and as a result, there was very little breakage and few instances of products getting crushed. So if he used an extra bag or two, no one ever complained. The bagger's name was Rick, and he and Ted got along famously.

They developed routines that amused the customers. For example, Ted would say, "Hey Rick, didja' hear about the guy who was stealing from the market while sitting on the shoulders of two vampires?" And Rick would answer, "Yeah, he was charged with shoplifting, on two counts." Or, Rick would start, "Hey Ted, I couldn't decide which pasta to buy . . ." And Ted would smack his head and say, "And then the penne dropped." Or if a shopper was young and had lettuce in her cart, Rick would put it in the bag and ask, "Are you planning to make a honeymoon salad?" And when the shopper looked confused, Ted would jump in, "Honeymoon salad, Lettuce alone." Another one that always got a groan from everyone in line: Rick would hold up a carton of milk and ask, "Do you want me to put this in a bag?" And before the shopper could respond, Ted would step in and say, "No, just leave it in the carton."

The banter amused the customers, or at least most of them, and many would wait in Ted's checkout line just for the amusement and also for the wine and food suggestions. Ted was enjoying his second career in marketing.

...

There was one older man who did not find the banter amusing. Whenever he went through Ted's line, and whenever Rick was bagging, the older man always found fault fault with Rick and never failed to mention it, sotto voce, so all the other customers could hear. His name was Marlin Pressler, and Ted could not remember ever seeing Marlin smile or say anything nice. Dour was an appropriate description. He would check the price of everything Ted scanned that appeared on the check-out screen and mumble under his breath about how much less food cost in the old days.

Marlin's nasty comments were hurtful to Rick, but Rick never responded. He just did his job. Once, when Rick put a carton of eggs on top of a bag of groceries so they would not be crushed, Marlin said, "Only a moron would put the eggs on top where they can fall out of the bag and break. Don't you know anything?" Rick apologized; that was simply the way he was. And he put an extra rubber band around the carton to keep the carton from opening. Ted just bit his tongue.

...

One Thursday morning, Ted noticed that Marlin, who was second in line, was pale, and he looked shaky and unwell. But then Ted returned his attention to his current customer and carried on his usual banter. Rick looked up from his bagging and also noticed that Marlin did not look right. He asked, "Mr. Pressler, are you OK?" "Of course I am OK, just mind your bagging. I'm just . . ."

As Ted turned around, Marlin crumpled to the floor and stopped breathing.

Ted, who was good in almost any situation, froze. But in a flash, Rick dropped to the floor next to Marlin. "Call 911," Rick said, and he started to administer CPR.

By the time the paramedics arrived, Marlin's eyes were open, and he was breathing, and everyone said it was Rick, the bagger, who had saved Marlin's life. The paramedics agreed as they loaded Marlin on a gurney to take him to the hospital.

...

After things returned to normal, or as normal as things could be, Ted turned to Rick and said, "That was amazing! You saved his life! How did you know how to do that?"

"I learned CPR my first year in medical school," Rick said, shyly.

Ted was taken aback. "You were in medical school?"

"Yes," Rick responded. "In my last year I was in a car accident and suffered extensive brain damage that put an end to my medical career before it even started."

"Wow!" was all Ted could come back with.

...

Several weeks went by, then one day a familiar face appeared in Ted's checkout line. It was Marlin. His color was good, and he looked surprisingly healthy. He was smiling shyly.

"Hey, Ted. Hey Rick," he said in a loud voice. "What do you call a grumpy old fool whose life you saved?"

And at exactly the same time, as if they had rehearsed it, Ted and Rick, replied, "911!" Marlin was a changed man. Rick was a hero. And Ted was really happy with his new career in marketing.

A Rare Glimpse
into the Obvious

WALTER HAD A GIFT, or perhaps it was a curse. He could sense when something was going to happen before it happened. It could be something as insignificant as knowing that in a few seconds the phone was going to ring and it would be aunt Becca, or something not so insignificant, such as knowing that a car on the freeway was going to suddenly spin out of control and cause a major pileup. But most of the time, it was the largely insignificant thing.

For example, once when he was at his aunt's and uncle's for Thanksgiving dinner, Walter suddenly broke out giggling. Everyone at the table looked at Walter, who shrugged then started giggling again. A minute later, Uncle Frank farted. Not a tiny fart. A big, loud, sustained, whoa-Nellie, everybody-into-the-life-boats fart. And then, of course, everybody at the table laughed. Except Uncle Frank. Uncle Frank did not know he was going to fart. Walter did.

Walter had a pretty good track record for knowing exactly what was coming in the day's mail. Often he could tell you the headline in the morning's *Herald Gazette*. He knew what song was coming up next on the radio or what commercial would be the next to interrupt "The Beverly Hillbillies."

He would tell his mom or dad not to answer the phone. Of course they would answer the phone anyway, and it would be someone selling insurance. Or the phone would ring, and Walter would say, "It's grandma," and when Walter's mom or dad picked up the phone, sure enough, it was grandma. It was like caller ID, in the days before caller ID.

Walter also knew what questions would be asked on his chemistry exam or his history exam, and he used this knowledge to be prepared with the correct answers. Consequently, he was a straight-A student, although he never told his classmates or his teachers about his talent. Walter knew they probably would have laughed and said, "No way!" And besides, he did study, so he wasn't really cheating. He just knew what was important and what was not. And more often than not, he studied the things that were not going to be asked on the exam because he was naturally curious.

...

One night when Walter's dad had the guys over for their weekly poker game, and Walter was walking through the room to get something to nosh while he was doing his homework, he passed the card table and knew his father would draw an Ace and a King. And wouldn't you know it, his dad drew an Ace of Hearts and a King of Clubs. Walter said nothing at the time, but after everyone had gone home, he confided to his dad that he had known he was going to draw a King and an Ace and win the pot.

Walter's dad was an attorney and knew that it was just as well that Walter kept his advance knowledge to himself. But he made a mental note that when Walter turned eighteen, maybe the two of them could take in some horseracing at the Oak Grove County Fair. Or better still, celebrate Walter's eighteenth with a trip to Las Vegas.

...

While Walter could accurately predict whether the next pitch would result in a fly ball, or a single, a double, or a home run, he could not predict the final score of the game or even the outcome of the inning. His insights were generally limited to the next specific event. And that probably was a good thing.

The temptation with such a gift was to use this foreknowledge to cheat, specifically at gambling, black jack, roulette, horse racing, and the like. But that would not be honest, and Walter had a strong sense of honor and fairness. Using his gift to cheat was simply not an option. Walter knew that to use his gift dishonestly might very well result in his gift being taken away.

...

One other thing Walter knew was that when he asked Penny Lange in the library for her phone number, she would give it to him. And that when he called and asked her to be his date at the senior prom, she would say yes. And that when he said at the prom the next song would be "A Nightingale Sang in Berkeley Square," Penny would be amazed. But Walter would shrug and say it was just a lucky guess. And that when, after dating Penny for over five years, and after Walter got his college degree in accounting, he would ask Penny to marry him, he knew she would say yes.

He never told Penny, but he knew she was pregnant before she did. And he knew the baby was a boy before the sonogram confirmed that it was. And of course, he knew they would name their son, Adam, after Penny's father.

Walter knew the offer he and Penny put in for the three-bedroom ranch style cottage that had just come on the market would be accepted. And it was. And Walter knew before he asked that his boss at the accounting firm would give him the raise that secured the mortgage on the house. For Walter it was all a rare glimpse into the obvious.

...

The years went by, pretty much exactly as Walter knew they would. Walter advanced in his job and was made vice president of the accounting firm. No surprise there. Nor was he surprised when Penny had their second child, Elizabeth, and they were able to afford that lovely two-story home on the outskirts of town.

...

Proud, without being hubristic, Walter and Penny wanted

to show off their new home and they offered to host Thanksgiving dinner at their new house. Everybody in the family accepted, as Walter was sure they would.

The turkey turned out perfectly as did the home-made cranberry sauce and mashed potatoes. And everybody, including Uncle Frank and Aunt Polly, was very impressed with the new house. Food was being passed around the table, the conversation was lively, and just as Walter knew they would, everybody was having one of the best Thanksgivings that anybody could remember. Until, for reasons nobody could have predicted, young Adam and Elizabeth started to giggle. And I am pretty sure, you can guess what happened next.

The Cat
Under *the* Stairs

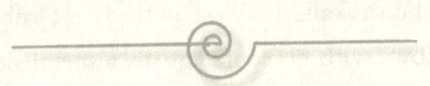

GUY AND MARINA MCGILL had been married almost ten years when the company Guy worked for transferred him to its San Francisco office. The move was eagerly anticipated because every summer Guy and Marina had visited their friends who lived in the Napa Valley when Guy and Marina went on their annual vacation. Now they would live there.

In preparation for their move, Marina took a flight to San Francisco and spent a week shopping for houses. She looked mostly in Marin County, just on the other side of the San Francisco Bay, where it was sunnier than in the city. San Francisco can be very foggy in summer, and gloomy, and depressing. Marin County was a lot warmer, like a very different country. Yet it was close enough to the city for work and less than an hour's drive from their friend's home in the Napa Valley wine country.

Marina looked at dozens of houses and culled the selection down to four that she and Guy could look at together with their agent when Guy flew up from Los Angeles the following weekend.

The house they both instantly fell in love with was designed by a young architect who had been a student of Frank Lloyd Wright at Taliesin West in Arizona. The home was a pastiche of Taliesin West with desert rubble pillars, corner windows with no center posts, a metal sloping roof, a low ceiling in the entry, the whole nine yards. And they could actually afford it — just — with Guy's pay raise and promotion.

In the tradition of Frank Lloyd Wright, the house was set just below the brow of a hill and looked out at the Petaluma River to the north and the top of the San Francisco Bay to the east. Looking south, they could just see the top of the fifty-two story Bank of America building in San Francisco. The hill on which the house was built was covered in oak trees. It was the home of their dreams.

...

Guy decided to acclimate their cat, Butternut, to the drive they would have to make from Southern California to their new home in the Bay Area. They called their cat Butternut because one of her hind legs had a patch of fur the color of butternut squash. And they called her Butter Nutter, Nuttzy, Butterofsky, and a half-dozen other affectionate names.

Guy put Butternut in his Datsun 280-Z, and the two went for long drives around the Los Angeles area. Butternut just curled up under the rear window and snoozed. How she would be on the drive north was anybody's guess.

...

The movers came a few weeks later and packed up the house and, the next day, Marina and Guy left in two separate cars for the six-hour drive to the Bay Area and to their new home. Butternut, who had been calm for most of the test drives Guy took her on, was not a happy camper, and she yowled and fussed for almost the entire trip. Guy tried singing to her, telling her amusing stories, giving her treats — which she refused — all while trying to focus his attention on driving the long journey on Interstate 5 through the center of the state, Marina following right behind all the way in their second car.

At exactly 6:37 PM, Marina and Guy pulled into the driveway of their new home. They unloaded their sleeping bags and the few provisions they had brought with them. These included several cans of cat food, a food bowl and a water bowl, a can opener, a bag of junk food, and a bottle of Champagne to celebrate their new home and their new life in Marin County, California. Butternut joined in and celebrated with a dish of tuna. All her protests apparently now forgiven.

...

Two days later the Bekins moving van pulled up to the house, and by evening all the furniture was in place and a mountain of moving boxes left to be unpacked. It was almost as if a light had gone on in Butternut's head when she was let out of the spare bedroom and she recognized all the furniture from the old house.

Marina who had worked in advertising in Los Angeles when she met Guy, had retired to spend her time weaving, a craft she was very good at. And there was a perfect bedroom for her loom that she claimed as her studio. But before she could take up her weaving again, she needed to get the boxes unpacked and the house pulled together.

While Marina unpacked, Butternut, who was now in her middle years, explored every inch of the house, and then she ventured outside, where she explored the hillside. There were so many new things to see and do.

At night, while the three of them watched TV in bed, they could hear the great horned owls in the oaks outside the bedroom and, from time to time, the sound of raccoons knocking over the trash cans. And a few times, they heard the howling of coyotes.

...

Guy was thrilled with the move and found living in the Bay Area suited him better than Southern California, where he always felt like a fish out of water. In the "City By The Bay," Guy could actually wear a wool sweater, even in summer. He enjoyed taking the ferry to work every morning and returning to the Larkspur Landing ferry terminal on the Marin County side of the bay in the evenings, from where it was a short drive home. Every day was like a mini-cruise. Once he even saw the conning tower of a submarine a few hundred feet to the west. The sub was probably leaving the Hunter's Point shipyard, where it had been in for repairs.

Guy's company had lockers and showers in the restrooms, and Guy brought his running gear and ran every day at lunch. He told Marina, "It is so incredible to run along the Embarcadero and see Alcatraz Island, the Golden Gate Bridge, and the Marin Headlands." He said he felt that every day was like he was on vacation. In San Francisco!

...

Marina and Guy added a path and a seating area under the oaks in their backyard, where on warm evenings they could sit with a glass of wine and watch the sun set to the west, Butternut always nearby.

A few years later, they added a raised-bed garden, where Marina could grow vegetables and flowers. And about the same time, they had a hen house built that would soon be populated by nine hens and a rooster. They named the chickens after operas or opera singers, including Luciano, the bantam rooster, and Carmina, the head hen. The hens, all of whom were young, were prodigious egg layers, and all the eggs they could not eat, Marina and Guy donated to the local food bank. They loved their life in Marin.

...

But sadly, as happens with all our beloved pets, Butternut

had grown old. She was fifteen now, and her health had been failing for some time. She had gone for a week without eating and barely drinking any water. The time had come.

When their vet knocked on the door, he was greeted by a tearful Marina and Guy. The vet, who was called Dr. Bob, came into the house and lovingly and compassionately eased Butternut into her next life. She was the "friendly kitty" that had sat on Marina's lap the first time Marina had come to visit Guy, just after they had met, and now Butternut was gone. Her death was hard on both Guy and Marina.

...

That spring, their close friend Jane, who lived in the Napa Valley, and whom Guy had known since their art school days, had a mom cat that had a litter of new kittens, and Marina and Guy went for a visit and to see if any of the kittens, whose eyes were not yet open, might find a home with them. As luck would have it, the litter contained two kittens, both calico/torties who had the color of butternut squash in their fur. And so just as soon as they were weaned, tiny Bernice and tiny Beatrix came to live with Marina and Guy. And once again, the house was filled with the joy of kittens. And, of course, there was the rite of passage when Beatrix and Bernice discovered the joys of pulling down an entire roll of toilet paper.

A year later, the kittens' cousin, an irresistible calico with a bob tail and a large patch of butternut squash-colored fur, Bobbin, joined the family. How could they say no? They couldn't.

...

Marina continued to weave, and her weaving was winning recognition, and she was getting invited to participate in some very prestigious shows. Guy continued to advance in his job and was made a vice president. And the house they could barely afford became a little easier to afford. This was good because they discovered early on that houses designed by — or in their case — in the tradition of Frank Lloyd Wright leaked like a sieve and required a lot of upkeep. A lot. And it seemed everything that needed fixing cost exactly twenty thousand dollars.

...

A stray male tabby cat began sleeping on the bales of straw that Marina used on the floor of the hen house, which by now had been modified several times and was proudly referred to as Chateau Le Coop. Marina put a notice on the community mailboxes asking if anyone knew to whom this odd gray and orange tabby cat belonged. It turned out that two neighbors who lived one street over had gotten a puppy, and their cat Wally had left home. The neighbors were only too happy for Marina and Guy to adopt him. And continuing with names that began with B, they called him Barnaby or, in honor of his previous name, Wallace Barnaby, a name that fit him to a T. Or a B, as it were.

In a period of a few years, the cat population had increased from one cat to two, three, and now four, and that was more cats than anybody needed. Until . . . .

...

Marin County averaged about forty inches of rainfall a year. And sometimes fifty inches or more in an El Niño year. During one of these seemingly endless El Niño rainy seasons, a handsome long-haired cat began taking shelter under the redwood stairs at the back of the house. Marina felt sad for the cat, and she wanted to adopt him and bring him in from the cold and rain. But Guy put his foot down and said, "No. Four cats is more than enough." And argue though Marina might, the decision was final. NO MORE CATS!

The rains went on and on, and the cat grew thin and shabby. His beautiful long fur became matted. It was pathetic to watch. And yet the cat was determined and showed no signs of going away. "You *will* come around and adopt me," he seemed to be saying.

...

One particularly gloomy day, when there was a break in the rain but the skies were still filled with clouds, Guy could not take the guilt anymore, and he broke down. Without Marina's knowledge, he took a bowl of dry cat food and pushed the bowl way under the redwood deck that was at the bottom of the stairs.

While he was pushing the bowl under the deck, Guy

heard a clink as the bowl bumped into another bowl. Bending down for a better look, he discovered a bowl just like the one he had shoved under the deck. And it too contained cat crunchies.

Hmm? He thought.

Later that day, he said to Marina, "Did someone we know put a bowl of cat food under the deck?"

To which Marina answered, "You must have been putting cat food under the deck yourself if you discovered my bowl." And they both burst out laughing, relieved that they were going to help this beautiful cat.

Because the cat took shelter under the redwood stairs that were just outside the back door of the house, they decided to call him Baxter, as in Back Stairs.

And so, they began putting the food at the top of the stairs, just outside the back door.

Then they would watch as Baxter crept cautiously across the redwood deck and up the stairs to the food bowl. If he caught sight of either Marina or Guy, he turned around and darted back down the stairs, across the deck, and down the hillside.

Over time, Baxter started to feel more confident, and one day when the rains had passed and the wisteria was in bloom, they saw something that was nothing short of miraculous: Baxter trotted up the stairs, and for the first time, his tail was held proudly in the air. Could it be this feral cat was starting to trust Marina and Guy?

...

Marina placed a wicker basket with a blanket on top, kind of like a tent or a cave, for Baxter to sleep in at night. It was on the landing just outside the back door. But would Baxter use it? They hoped so. His beautiful long fur was still very matted and shabby. But he had started to put on weight. He now approached the stairs with more confidence, and then one evening, Marina and Guy saw him go into the basket. And this became his nightly bed and in the afternoon sometimes, too.

One day, Marina opened the door and laid down near where Baxter was snoozing in his covered basket cave and, very, very gently, she put her hand on his flank. He growled a warning softly, and she withdrew her hand. But she continued to lie within a few feet of the cat, and the cat did not move. They were cautiously getting to know one another. Marina repeated this routine several more times, and finally the growl was replaced by tentative purring.

...

Their vet, Dr. Bob, suggested bringing Baxter in for a check up to make sure he did not have any diseases that might affect the other cats in the household. Marina placed Baxter's food bowl in the back of a Havahart™ trap, and after a half dozen unsuccessful tries, his hunger gave way to caution, and she managed to lure Baxter into the trap and off to the vet.

At the vet's office, Baxter was anaesthetized and shampooed, and his matted fur was trimmed off, revealing his fine colorings: gray and white with just a few accents of butternut squash-colored fur.

Dr. Bob gave Baxter several tests and pronounced him healthy and without any communicable feline diseases. He gave Baxter a host of shots and changed his status from "intact male" to "neutered." And when the anesthesia wore off and Baxter was ready to go home, Dr. Bob told Marina, "This is a beautiful Maine Coon cat. He is healthy and about two years old. My best guess is he was either abandoned or had gotten lost. But I am happy to see this fine boy now has a happy home."

Then Dr. Bob grew serious, and he cautioned Marina. He said, "When you get him home and let him out of the trap, be aware that you may never see him again."

...

Marina brought Baxter back home. She placed the trap on the landing at the top of the back stairs and opened the door. Baxter, like a ball out of a canon, shot out and in a flash was down the steps, across the deck, and down the hill, and out of sight. All they could do, Marina told Guy when she called him at work to relate the events of the morning, was hope. And Guy, trying to be positive, said that at the very least, Baxter now had gotten his shots, and they had done the best they could.

When Guy got home that afternoon from work, he found Marina by the back door, waiting. "Baxter's not come back?" he asked. "No, and I am just heartsick!" she said. "Did we do the right thing? What if we never see him again? I don't think I could take it," she continued.

And then, as Guy was trying to reassure Marina that they had done the right thing, they saw Baxter bound up the stairs with his tail held high and stop right in front of his food bowl. And he ate, and ate, and ate. And while he may not have forgiven Marina and Guy, he did not appear to be holding a grudge either.

...

Over the following months, Baxter moved in and joined the other four cats in the household. The other four cats were territorial at first, but eventually they accepted the new cat on the block, just as in turn they had been accepted. And like the other four cats, Baxter now wore a magnet around his neck that magically opened the cat door next to the kitchen.

For a large cat — Baxter was bigger than any of the other cats — he was totally intimidated by the hens, especially by Carmina, who would give Baxter the stink eye when they crossed paths. And Baxter would avert his gaze. It was humorous, a red hen intimidating this big burly Maine Coon cat. But everybody managed to get along.

...

Over the years, one by one, the cats died off, and it was very hard on Marina and Guy every time they had to have one of the cats euthanized. They buried each of their cats on the property, along with a finch, a canary, a hawk, and numerous hens and a rooster.

Then it was down to Barnaby, who by now, was some-where in his twenties, and Baxter who was still a youth-ful thirteen.

And then, it was just Baxter.

Because Barnaby had adopted Marina and Guy, they never knew exactly how old he was. He might even have been as old as twenty-four. Methuselah might have been a more appropriate name.

...

Baxter was the most companionable of all their cats, perhaps with the exception of Butternut. But he was, at the very least, on a par with Butternut. He sat on Guy's lap while Marina and Guy watched TV, and he would fre-quently meow to comment on something he liked. He paid rapt attention when Guy and Marina watched "Wild King-dom," and especially when Marlin Perkins and "Wild Kingdom" featured cats of any size. Then when they turned off the TV and went to bed, Baxter slept between Marina and Guy, between the pillows at the top of the bed, where Marina would sometimes place her hand underneath the happily sleeping cat, who would instantly start to purr.

In the morning Baxter would enthusiastically follow Guy into the kitchen when Guy put up the coffee, and he would sit with Marina and Guy while Guy read aloud to them in the library.

Baxter was eternally grateful to the people who rescued

him from the rains and wind and who had given him a life that was more than he could have ever hoped for. Marina said that he was the cat of a lifetime.

...

But one day, Marina remarked that Baxter did not seem himself. Something was missing from his usual spirit. It was hard to pinpoint, but something was just not right.

Marina took Baxter to Dr. Bob, and she explained that he just was not thriving. It was hard to explain, just an intuition. And sadly her observation was correct. After a series of tests, Dr. Bob gave Marina and Guy the bad news: Baxter had inoperable colon cancer. He might live a few more months, but the end was near. All they could do was give him as much love as possible and make him comfortable in his final days. And they did, for every remaining day of his life. He was the cat of a lifetime. And then, he was gone.

...

The house was incredibly empty. There was no Baxter on the bed or Baxter meowing in the morning when Guy put up the coffee. No Baxter to sit on a lap and purr. He was gone. And Marina and Guy thought their hearts would never heal.

...

Several months passed, and as fortune would have it, their good friend Jane in Napa Valley called and announced her mom cat — this must have been mom cat number seven or eight — had a new litter of kittens, and there were two who might be a perfect fit for Marina and Guy.

"Well," said Guy, "It can't hurt to look, can it?"

And as it turned out, Chloe and Chrysanthemum — Marina and Guy had moved on from B names into the Cs — two adorable calico kittens, each with a strip of butter-nut-squash coloring in their fur, came to live in Marin County in the house that was built by a student of Frank Lloyd Wright. But as much as Guy and Marina came to love the new kittens, who were so joyful and so into everything, they never forgot, not even for one moment, Baxter, the cat who had lived under the back stairs.

The Meek Shall
Inherit *the* Earth

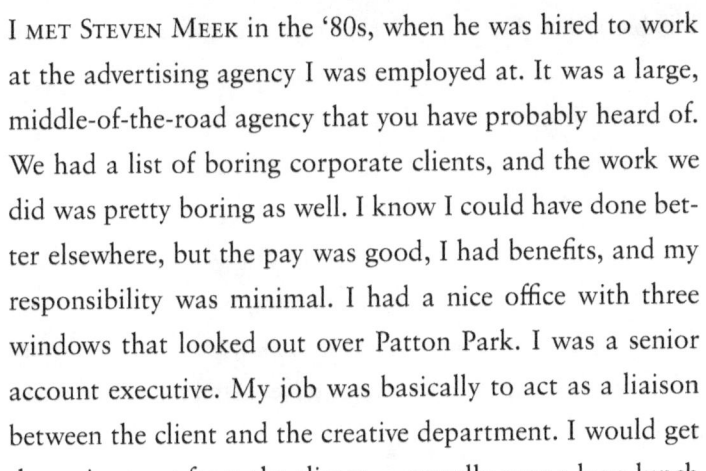

I met Steven Meek in the '80s, when he was hired to work at the advertising agency I was employed at. It was a large, middle-of-the-road agency that you have probably heard of. We had a list of boring corporate clients, and the work we did was pretty boring as well. I know I could have done better elsewhere, but the pay was good, I had benefits, and my responsibility was minimal. I had a nice office with three windows that looked out over Patton Park. I was a senior account executive. My job was basically to act as a liaison between the client and the creative department. I would get the assignment from the clients — usually over a long lunch at the agency's expense — and I would take the assignment back to the agency and brief the creative team. The creative team would create some ads or TV commercials that I would then take back and present to the client.

When Steven Meek was fresh out of art school and looking for his first job in advertising, Kate Lewiston, an advertising placement specialist, looked at his portfolio and observed, "Well, honey, you're not going to set the world on fire, but I am sure we can find you something." And it appears she was correct. We hired Steven as a junior art director.

Steven Meek turned out to be a hard-working, diligent, and reliable art director. Management liked Steven Meek because he always volunteered to take the assignments no one else wanted. He was known for always meeting his deadlines and for his meticulous attention to detail. Most important to the agency's partners, he always turned in his billable hours. He was not the most creative art director in the world of advertising; however, that was about to change.

But I'm getting ahead of myself.

Steven Meek kept to himself. While most of his colleagues in the creative department were going out for three-hour lunches, Steven Meek usually brought his lunch from home and spent his lunch hour reading *Advertising Age* and fantasizing about being one of those lauded creatives whose office walls are lined with major advertising awards, statues, and plaques.

Steven Meek was shy. He had a boyish look and was about ten pounds overweight. He wasn't fat; he was just a little pudgy. It was something he was not happy about.

A friend who lived in the same apartment building as Steven suggested he get an exercise bike. The friend said it was an inexpensive and easy way to shed a few pounds and get into shape.

Steven Meek did a little research and settled on an X-Cursion-250XL, which he ordered from a catalog and had shipped to the office. While the others would be out at lunch schmoozing and boozing, Steven Meek was going to work at getting into better shape and losing a few pounds.

...

The receptionist called Steven Meek and asked him to come pick up the large package just delivered by UPS. He did so promptly and brought the box back to his office. He waited until noon when the department had cleared out for lunch and the secretaries were in the conference room eating their lunches and watching "Days of Our Lives." He opened the box and, in short time, had the X-Cursion-250XL assembled and set up in the corner of his office, away from the door.

The X-Cursion-250XL was compact and did not take up much room. It had a knob for incrementally adjusting the tension, a cable-driven speedometer and odometer, plus a stop watch for determining elapsed time.

Steven Meek climbed aboard and gave it a test ride. Even at the lowest tension setting, he was breathing heavily after only five minutes. But he was determined. Over the following weeks, he went from the lowest tension setting of 1 all the way to the highest tension setting of 10. He increased his workout time from twenty to thirty minutes and then up to forty-five minutes per session. Before he knew it, the odometer displayed five hundred miles. And best of all, he had lost three pounds.

Steven Meek also discovered, though now he remembered his neighbor had also suggested it, that he could pedal backwards and the odometer and speedometer would continue to register. This was good for his upper leg muscles. So, he would pedal forward for ten minutes, then pedal backward for ten minutes, and then forward again, and then backward. He got so he could make the transition from forward to backward without missing a beat. He was starting to feel healthier and more confident about himself.

...

To pass the time while on the X-Cursion-250XL, Steven Meek sketched in his sketchpad, which he held in one hand while he sketched with his Pentel in the other hand. Drawing was one of his favorite classes at art school. That and design. With one eye on the elapsed time and the other on the page, he sketched elaborate still lifes, figure studies, logos, whatever came to mind. The pages in his sketchbook began to fill up. Occasionally he would come up with concepts for some of his accounts, but those ideas were never that great.

Sometimes Steven Meek would watch his speed increase and decrease on the speedometer. He got so he could pedal at a specific speed consistently, 14.5 MPH or 17.25 MPH.

And then something totally unexpected happened. While sustaining 18.5 MPH for twenty seconds, Steven Meek had a break-through idea for his new account, Obsidian Copy Toner, named Obsidian because the toner produced extraordinarily solid black prints. The headline, "It Looks Good on

Paper" popped into his head, and he reached for his sketch pad and jotted down this headline and then sketched a rough layout of how it might look as a magazine ad.

When his copywriter partner, Eric Danville, retuned from lunch, Steven Meek showed him the layout. "Damn!" Eric Danville said, "That's not too bad! Work up the layout, and I'll go write some copy, and we'll present it to the suits." ("Suits" was how the creative people referred to us, the account executives, because we wore suits like grownups while they dressed in jeans and t-shirts like kids.)

Steven Meek sat at his drawing board and worked up the layout. For a visual, he showed a side-by-side comparison of ordinary copy toner, which was kind of grey, and then the really black Obsidian toner using the Obsidian logo for the side-by-side comparison. The client loved it, and just like that, Steven Meek became a hero. OK, a minor hero, but a hero nonetheless.

...

Over the coming weeks, Steven Meek experimented with different speeds on his X-Cursion-250XL, but 18.5 MPH sustained for twenty seconds seemed to tap directly into his right brain. If he continued at 18.5 MPH for a longer time, more concepts and often better ones came into his head. The X-Cursion-250XL was not only doing wonders for his weight, it was also doing wonders for his career.

Out of curiosity, Steven Meek wondered what would happen if he pedaled backwards at 18.5 MPH. Pedaling backward at this speed took more effort and concentration but amazingly, the effect was even more powerful. Six concepts for six separate accounts, like an electric shock, shot into his brain, and he was having a hard time writing them all down.

...

The agency entered some of Steven Meek's and Eric Danville's ads in a regional advertising competition. The agency never won anything, although it always entered ads in every category. So everyone was thrilled when the agency finally won a handful of silver medals and one gold. And the agency entered some more important shows and took home some more awards, even a Best of Show in a competition that "nobody ever won." And all the award-winning ads were created by Steven Meek and Eric Danville.

As the awards and recognition increased, Steven Meek started getting better accounts for himself and Eric Danville to work on. Basically, Steven Meek was now, by far, more creative than his partner, though to be fair, Eric Danville was able to pay off Steven Meek's concepts with some very tight and well-crafted copy. They made a good team.

Steven Meek and Eric Danville were not only the hottest team in the agency, they were getting recognition as the hottest team in the business. On the strength of the outstanding creative work they were producing and the awards they were accruing, the agency started picking up new business, including a European car manufacturer, a regional airline, the fourth-largest bank in the US, and a national taco fast-food chain. Along with the new business came new job titles … Senior Creative Group Heads — and with the new titles came hefty bonuses and raises almost into the six figures.

…

The dynamic duo started getting phone calls from the top headhunters asking them to lunch to talk of bigger and better jobs with bigger and better agencies. Steven Meek even got a gushing phone call from Kate Lewiston, the headhunter who said that he would never set the world on fire when he was just out of art school. He reminded Kate Lewiston of what she had said, but she claimed not to remember ever saying such a thing. She said she always knew he was very talented and told everyone that he would be big someday, and she begged Steven Meek to let her represent him. He not-so-politely declined and hung up on Kate Lewiston. In fact Steven Meek and Eric Danville declined all the lucrative offers because the senior partners in the agency knew that geese who could lay golden eggs were worth every penny, and they were paying them handsomely and giving them all the best accounts to keep them from straying.

…

Word of the secret to Steven Meek's creative success had to get out sometime, and it did. No one was sure who leaked the story to the trade press, but *AdWeek* ran a long article and mentioned the possible connection between the exercise bicycle and Steven Meek's incredible burst of creativity.

Soon, X-Cursion-250XLs started appearing in offices all over town and all over the country. Creative teams were eschewing the long three-martini lunch in favor of pedaling their way to advertising fame and fortune. Statistically, however, the difference in the creativity for the advertising produced was marginal at best. It seemed only to work for one person, and that person never revealed the secret of the sustained speed of 18.5 MPH. So unless a creative person accidentally hit the magic sweet spot, the breakthrough creativity just was not there. But of course, this did not stop every agency from claiming that it did. And who knows? Steven Meek's X-Cursion-250XL might just have been a one-off.

...

Now that Steven Meek was at the height of his success, he decided to get rid of the X-Cursion-250XL and upgrade to the Lamborghini of stationary bicycles, the Vello d'Oro Eccellente. He donated his X-Cursion-250XL to the Goodwill, though he probably could have sold it for a fortune.

Steven Meek was long overdue for a vacation, which the partners of the agency agreed to pay for and which took him to Italy, and then to England, and later to France. It was a fine vacation, and not once did Steven Meek think about the advertising business or his agency. He took in the sights, and he soaked up the sun and the culture. He thought he could get very used to being a tourist. But eventually, the vacation was over, and Steven Meek returned to the agency.

...

While he was still on vacation, the Vello d'Oro Eccellente arrived, and the box was awaiting him in his new six-window corner office. He waited until lunchtime and then lovingly unpacked and set up the new bike. He was keen to hop on and test it out, but a meeting that had been put off until his return was scheduled in the conference room, and his presence was mandatory. And after that meeting, there was a department meeting and a dozen or two phone calls he needed to answer, so he never got to break in his new bike that day. Or the next, when he was away from the office all day at a TV commercial shoot.

Finally on Thursday, he climbed aboard the Vello d'Oro Eccellente. He used the real leather straps to secure his feet to the pedals, adjusted the digital dial to simulate a vigorous thirty-minute ride in the Swiss Alps, selected some spirited Alpine music from the bike's built-in stereo system, and away he went.

The quality of the bike's mechanism was responsive and elegant. He could feel the precision in the machine and experience the almost-total quiet of the pedaling. It was the most sensuous experience Steven Meek had ever had. It was almost spiritual. It bordered on erotic.

He slowly, very, very slowly, worked his way to 10 MPH, and then 12 MPH, and then, in a burst of speed, up to 18.5 MPH, his magical creative speed. It was exhilarating! It was fantastic! It was . . . NOTHING! Not a single idea popped into Steven Meek's head. If anything, instead of a wealth of creative ideas, there was absolutely nothing.

More than a bit apprehensive, Steven Meek reversed direction and started pedaling backwards, 8, 10, 13, 15, 16, 18, 18.1, 18.2, 18.3, and 18.5 MPH. The only thing that popped into his head was that he had forgotten to pay the electric bill. That was it. Not another breakthrough idea. Oh, there was one idea, a headline, "Tastes Great," for the fast-food taco account. And he knew that was way too expected to record.

Frantically he tried slowly increasing and decreasing his speed, pedaling first forward then backward. Nothing. Worse than nothing. Nada. Zip. Zilch. Not one thing.

...

Steven Meek did have one thought, "I have to get the X-Cursion-250XL back. Whatever the cost. I'll pay anything they ask. Whoever they might be."

He called the Goodwill, and spoke to the supervisor, and explained that he was the guy who brought in the X-Cursion-250XL exercise bike a month ago and, by any chance, was it still there? Or if not, did they have any record of who purchased it? The supervisor did remember the bike and said it was odd. The bike had not sold. Nobody even seemed to notice it. And then early last week, a young man came in and purchased the bike. Paid cash. Said something about having just been hired at a downtown advertising agency. And that was all he could remember.

...

This all happened a decade ago. Steven Meek dropped off the face of the earth, and nobody knew where he had gone or what he was doing. Or even if he was still working in advertising. Around the time Steven Meek dropped off the radar, I did hear of a new wunderkind in town who was suddenly the hot new art director. But I did not give it a second thought.

I retired shortly thereafter and lost contact with the people I had worked with. I did take a part-time job at an upscale wine shop in the Ironwood Mall, working as a sales associate. It kept me busy, and I got a very hefty discount on all of the best wines we carried.

So you can imagine my amazement when I looked up to see a familiar face come through the door of the wine shop. It was Steven Meek. He looked older, but he also looked fit, and my guess was he spent a lot of time at the gym.

We shook hands, and I said we definitely had some catching up to do. Steven Meek agreed and asked if I remembered Kate Lewiston. I said, "You mean the head-hunter who said you would never amount to much?" He said, "The very one. Except now she is Kate Meek. We've been married for ten years! In fact, I came in to buy a bottle of Champagne to celebrate our anniversary."

I was pleasantly amused to hear this and, while we were walking over to the sparkling wines section, I said, "How did this come about? I thought you really detested her."

Steven Meek laughed. He said, "Well, after I left the agency, I obviously needed to find a new job. It was by the sheerest luck that I was invited to a party a friend was throwing, and who should I run into at the party but Kate Lewiston! We did not know a lot of other people, and so we reluctantly began talking to each other.

"It turns out we knew a lot of people in common and even shared many of the same views. I asked her out, she accepted, and the rest is history.

We have two really great kids, a boy and a girl, and a nice home in McKinley Park, very close to the school. Oh, and here's the best part: Kate got me the interview at the company I have been working at for the last nine years. Remember X-Terra, the company that made my legendary X-Cursion-250XL exercise bike?" "Sure," I said, who could forget that?" "Well," Steven Meek said, "I'm the Senior Vice President, Director of Marketing for X-Terra!"

How unexpected was that?

Steven Meek selected a bottle of Gruet Blanc de Noirs, a lovely sparkling wine made in New Mexico of all places, but one of our better sellers. We shook hands and promised to stay in touch. As he was leaving, Steven Meek gave me his goofy grin and said, "If you ever need an exercise bicycle, call me. I can get you a very creative deal!"

Computer Crimes
of the Heart

———⟲———

Samantha was looking at the local news on the *Hazelridge Herald* website, something she did only once a day because the "late breaking news" broke, as it were, only once a day — and often late in the day. She was reading an article about someone who had hacked into Hazelridge High School's computer server and posted the grades for the finals for the entire sophomore class — even for those students who had received Ds and Fs — on the home page of the Hazelridge High School website.

But that was nothing. The hacker also posted a series of photos of the football coach having sex standing up in a stall in the coaches' locker room with the girls' Phys Ed coach. The photos were posted just below the sophomore class's finals grades. This hack caused a scandal not seen in the sleepy bedroom town of Hazelridge since the town treasurer was arrested after embezzling a half a million dollars and attempting to leave the country.

The hack was discovered by the computer science teacher, Arnie Green, who also served as IT director for the school. According to Green, the hacker knew what he or she, though probably he, was doing. And because the grades posted were those of the sophomore class, the suspect was in all likelihood a sophomore at Hazelridge High.

There was no immediate comment from the principal's office. The two coaches had been put on administrative leave pending an investigation by the Hazelridge School Board. The author of the *Hazelridge Herald* article also revealed that the football coach's wife had filed for divorce, revealing to the author that her soon-to-be-ex-husband was a pathetic lover with "undersized equipment," and she felt sorry for the girls' Phys Ed coach, who was just out of college and who was not only going to lose her job but was inheriting a "loser" of a man who never picked up his clothes, or helped around the house, and was a complete slob. The coach's soon-to-be-ex-wife added that she and her three kids wished dad good riddance! And she wished the girl's Phys Ed coach GOOD LUCK, saying, "Honey, you're really going to need it!"

...

Samantha was amused as she read the details of the report of the hacking and the resulting suspension of Coach Miller, the football coach, and Coach Gifford, the girl's Phys Ed coach. She loathed Ms. Gifford, who was mean and sarcastic and never let an opportunity pass to remind Samantha what a total spaz she was. Coach Gifford frequently chided Samantha, saying "If you're afraid of being hit by a volleyball, how in God's name are you going to cope with everything else life can and will throw at you?"

Coach Miller, the football coach, was known and loathed by everyone as a total douchebag, including by the entire varsity football team he coached. A team that was as much of a loser as Coach Miller himself: 0 for 11 last season was considered a good year. At least the team showed up.

Samantha knew who the hacker was. It was Willy Craster, her next-door neighbor and boyfriend of sorts. In fact it was Samantha who encouraged Willy to post those photos and grades in the first place. Willy and Sam were juniors, kind of misfits, but very bright misfits, and intentionally listed the grades for the sophomore class to throw Mr. Green off their trail.

Samantha hung out almost every day after school at Willy's house, in his bedroom, where they did their homework together and shared a kiss or two and the very occasional grope, but only if Sam initiated it.

Samantha would try out different fragrances on Willy and ask his opinion, which was always the same, "Uh, yeah, I like it, I guess." Samantha would wear tight shorts and loose tank tops that revealed some of her boobs when she bent over in front of Willy but, sadly, this was a mostly wasted effort. If she had walked into Willy's room totally naked, it would probably go unnoticed. Hacking the Hazelridge High website was Sam's idea as a way of getting closer to Willy, but hacking, it would appear, was the only thing that turned him on.

Willy was a classic nerd and something of a computer genius. Hacking into a server as poorly protected as Hazelridge High School's computer — Password: Hazelridge123 — was something he could do in his sleep. Willy and Samantha spent endless hours roaming the contents of the server, specifically the individual teachers' computers, which is where they found the intimate photos — selfies actually — of Coach Miller and Coach Gifford. They also found a stash of pornography on Coach Miller's computer, which they planned to reveal as soon as the current posting lost traction. The personal emails between the teachers at Hazelridge were also a possibility for a future post.

...

It took Willy about ten minutes to crack the new "more secure, password: Hazelridge123456.

Samantha was physically aroused by the cache of pornographic photos they had uncovered on Coach Miller's computer. Willy did not seem to notice. Samantha wondered what she would have to do to get Willy's attention. She was an attractive, healthy, young woman. Guys said she had a great bod. She had long, curly, reddish-brown hair and large, brilliant, blue eyes. Most guys would fall all over her. But not Willy. Willy spent ninety-eight percent of his time looking at his computer and, at most, two percent of his time looking blankly at Samantha.

She had done everything she could to get Willy to pay attention to her and give her more than just a timid peck on the lips. So why was Willy not falling all over her like those other guys, the guys she really had no interest in?

Then an idea struck.

"Willy?" Samantha said.

"What, Sam?" Willy responded, not looking up from his computer.

"Willy, will you teach me to hack?"

Willy was suddenly alert and excited. "Sure," he said and turned to look directly at Samantha. "Are you really serious?"

Willy found the notion that Samantha was interested in computers caused a stirring in his body that was not at all expected. And perhaps for the first time, he saw Samantha as something other than his geeky next-door neighbor whom he had known since they were kids. And, now that he thought about it, she was kind of sexy. Maybe even majorly sexy. Why had he never noticed this until now? And for the first time, he noticed how sexy her curly hair smelled. Willy was gobsmacked!

...

And so over the next few weeks, as soon as they finished their homework, Willy pulled up a chair and sat very close to Samantha as he imparted everything he knew about breaking into another computer. And as Willy instructed Samantha, their legs touching because of the closeness of the two chairs, Samantha could hear Willy's breathing, which was heavier than his usual breathing. Was he finally noticing her?

...

Willy said it was time for Sam's first solo hack. After some discussion, it was decided Samantha would hack into Arnie Green's computer. Arnie was the computer science teacher who, incidentally, had given Samantha a D in his Computer Basics class and suggested she never go near a computer again. He had snickered and said she could not tell a one from a zero. And Arnie Green was the one who had discovered the hack of the school's computer. Willy said he thought Mr. Green was a total dork who could not find his ass with both hands. Sam thought this comment was hysterical, and they both laughed. So Arnie Green would be their next target, and Sam would take the lead.

...

Samantha quickly discovered the same lame password that Willy had discovered, but this time all on her own, and she was quickly into the Hazelridge High School server. From there she slipped effortlessly through the loosest of security firewalls and into Arnie Green's computer, which was protected by an equally lame password: g0LDenONe.

"Sheesh," said Samantha. "What a total dipshit!"

Willy laughed. Sam's observation did not surprise him at all, and he was impressed with how quickly Samantha broke Arnie Green's password. And now that he was paying attention, how could he have missed the really cute way she scrunched her nose when she was navigating the files on the server? He had to resist the urge to just grab and ravish her.

...

"Willy!" Samantha yelled.

"I'm right here, Sam, no need to shout," said Willy.

"Check this out. Green has a folder for every teacher in the school, and he has been keeping a copy of all their personal emails! Even Coach Miller's and Coach Gifford's. And look! He even has a "CONFIDENTIAL" folder for Mrs. Angleton!" Ursula Angleton was the high school principal. "What do you suppose he has in that folder, Willy?"

Willy was lost. He was absorbed in the nape of Samantha's long, slender neck which was revealed because she had tied her hair back in a ponytail. And there was something so erotic about her ears!

Without waiting for an answer, Samantha opened the "U. Angleton: Confidential" folder. Nested inside were dozens of sub-folders that she was scrolling down through.

Willy's attention now was focused on Sam's hands as she moved the mouse, then her long, lovely, sensuous fingers as she keyed in commands. He was fantasizing those hands on his bod . . . .

...

"WILLY!" Samantha shouted, finally bringing Willy back into the moment. There's a folder called MI AMOR and it contains email love letters between Mrs. Angleton and Mr. Green!

Wow, I can't believe this, Willy listen to this!"

Samantha read a long and seductively vivid email from Mrs. Angleton revealing in graphic detail how Arnie Green had seduced her after the faculty meeting, in her office, where they had gone allegedly to find a book she wanted Arnie to read. The email was dated from a little over a year ago.

Hearing the explicit details of how Mrs. Angleton was receptive to Mr. Green's advances and how she had dreamed about this moment for years and how she had yearned for him to tear off her dress and ravage her body and, and, and . . . . It was too much for Willy.

He grabbed Samantha up out of her chair and kissed her passionately. Tongues and all. Samantha swooned and allowed herself to be thrown onto Willy's bed, and what *she* had fantasized for all these months, finally happened. And it happened again. And once more before they were stopped by Willy's mom, who shouted up the stairs, "What in God's name is going on up there?" Oops!

...

The email exchange between the principal and Mr. Green appeared the next day on the Hazelridge High School home page. Both parties strenuously denied the email exchange and blamed it all on the over-active imagination of the Hazelridge High Hacker. Mr. Green left town and was not heard from again. And Mrs. Angleton joined Mr. Miller and Ms. Gifford on administrative leave until the

Hazelridge School Board could get to the bottom of who had been doing what to whom. And why.

The Hazelridge High Hacker was never caught. Except by Samantha. And just for the record, it's the Hazelridge High Hackers.

Honest Abbie

FOR A SHADY BUSINESS LIKE ADVERTISING, where the truth and the facts are rare commodities, sometimes honesty can be the best policy.

I worked in the business for several decades, and I feel qualified to make this comment. And I'll be the first to admit that I stretched a fact or two in my days. Maybe even two or three hundred facts. Probably more. I stopped counting. Isn't that what advertising is all about? And who's counting?

So when I meet someone honest and straightforward, more often than not, it's the exception, not the rule.

Abbie Green was one of these rare people. She was hired at my agency as a junior copywriter. It was her first job right out of college. She was young, bright, a great dresser, and in time she turned out to be a very excellent copywriter. We were partnered on several projects early in her career. I was an art director and had been in the business for just under ten years. I was amazed at how quickly Abbie learned the craft. She knew pretty much everything I knew, and *she* had only been working in advertising for six months.

Our supervisor was Ellen Blunt, a senior copywriter who had been in advertising a few years more than I had. She was a no-nonsense copywriter who could crank out thirty-second TV scripts in her sleep: twenty-eight seconds with a two-second pull-up, sixty words max. Her writing was not flashy, but it was tight and got in every point.

When it came to mentoring Abbie, Ellen Blunt was a stern taskmaster.

Abbie would bring her copy — that's what we call the words that appear in a magazine advertisement or TV commercial — to Ellen who would read the copy, never commenting on whether it was good or bad. And with her long slender finger, Ellen would tap her manicured fingernail in the middle of the copy and say, "Start here. Start in the middle." And Abbie would take the copy back to her office — well *office* is really an overstatement, converted closet is more like it, because Abbie could not even close the door fully the space was so tight. And Abbie would put a fresh sheet of paper in her typewriter and turn out a better piece of copy. Did I say she was a quick study?

Abby used to joke, give me five minutes and I'll give you an ad. Give me ten minutes and I'll give you a better ad.

Coming up with effective advertising concepts is a mysterious process. You get your assignment and appropriate research materials, you identify your demographic target or targets, and you agree on a strategy. And then you create advertising based on that strategy. But that's all left-brain material. There's more to the creative process.

My theory is you have to trick your right brain — the creative side of your brain — into thinking you are not trying to come up with anything creative. So you go about your daily life, and when the right brain is ready, it cuts in and lets you know. Like the way sometimes you get an idea when you are driving or in the shower. The right side of your brain is always working in the background.

The creative team, the art director and the copywriter, spend much of the day sitting in one or the other's office, talking about this and that, looking through old advertising awards annuals for inspiration, but spending almost no time on the assignment. You wind up getting to know the other person pretty well. Abbie, I learned, was recently married to a hot-shot art director at another ad agency. I had met him once or twice, nice-enough guy. And Abbie learned all about my divorce and my problems getting my ex to let me spend time with my two kids. Chit chat. Lots of chit chat.

Abbie had a wicked sense of humor too and loved to tell jokes. She was good at it. On this one particular assignment, she was right in the middle of a joke when she stopped abruptly and said, "Hey, what if the car rear ends a flying saucer stopped on the freeway, and the bottle falls onto the floor, but it doesn't spill?" The bottle Abbie was referring to was the innovative packaging for the soft drink account we were working on. The bottle that wouldn't spill and was designed for drinking on the run. And just like that, it's off to the races. Ideas start to percolate up from the right brain and, before you know it, an ad or TV commercial is conceived. As I said, it's a mysterious process.

...

Abbie was especially good at working with very technical information and simplifying it so it could be communicated clearly and in a few words. I used to kid her and say "Abbie, you can turn a mountain of bullshit into a molehill of bullshit." I think she was flattered. More likely, she thought it was a dumb remark, but she was too polite to say so.

...

A project that neither one of us will ever forget was an advertorial we created for a client and that appeared in *National Geographic* magazine. An advertorial is an advertisement that is designed to look like an actual article in the magazine. Usually the text *ADVERTISEMENT* appears in very tiny type at the top of each page, but most people don't see it. The idea is that the reader believes the ad is actually an article in the publication, which gives credibility to the ad's message.

We had the assignment to create an advertorial for Adkin's Wild Animal Park, a chain of wild animal theme parks across the country. The company used the money from admissions to its parks for research into animal conservation. Adkin's had successfully bred two giant pandas in captivity in its Minnesota park and wanted to use this story to sell interest in its wild animal parks. And this was perfect for Abbie. The client sent over a mountain of technical research that Abbie ploughed through and condensed into a splendid little molehill of information that became a really excellent story the whole family would be enthralled with. The client had also provided some beautiful photographs for us to include in the advertorial.

...

The advertorial was put together with photos and typeset text, logos, headlines, and subheads. We had everything in place except for one subhead that Adkin's was supposed to send over as soon as their marketing team had revised it. As a placeholder until we got the actual copy for the subhead, I added what we call greek copy — because as the saying goes, 'it looks like Greek to me' — something like "Ollo cholo nextum dilsop unam." When the Adkin's team sent over the revised subhead, then the Greek copy would be replaced. The only problem was the client forgot to send over the new subhead copy, and we all forgot about the subhead with the greeked copy.

The ad was passed around our agency and the client for approval, and each of us who was involved in the project initialed the stamped approval box on the back. This approval included the client and his staff; Robert, our creative director; the account executive; Ellen Blunt, our supervisor; and of course Abbie and me. Signed off by all concerned, the advertorial production material was printed and then sent to *National Geographic* where it was inserted into the magazine.

...

The edition of *National Geographic* hit the newsstands and, as they say, the shit hit the fan. The account executive in charge of Adkin's Wild Animal Park came storming into the creative department and, to our chagrin, showed us the ad with the greek subhead there for all to see. He had just gotten off the phone with the client, who was furious, as well he should have been.

A group had been summoned in front of the creative department secretary's desk that included Robert, the creative director who was in charge of everything creative that was done in the department; of course Ellen Blunt, our supervisor; the account executive; the production department; and Abbie and me. All of us had added our initials when the final ad was shown to us for approval. I should point out that the client and his staff had also signed off on the ad.

Robert was not a happy camper. He asked who was responsible for this mistake. The silence was deafening. When not one person responded, Abbie held up her hand and said, "I guess that would be me. I was the writer, and the responsibility is mine. I should have caught that error, and I didn't."

Robert sternly looked directly at Abbie and said,

"Abbie, I want to see you in my office in fifteen minutes." Ellen Blunt and everyone else disappeared into their offices as if a skunk had backed into the hallway with his tail lifted. And everyone sighed a heavy sigh of relief. Everyone that is except Abbie. I felt bad. It really was my fault. I was the senior member of the team but, hey, I needed the job so I could pay child support to the ex.

Abbie later confided to me that she was certain this mistake was the end of her brief advertising career. She knew she would be fired for sure. She said she went into the ladies restroom and splashed cold water on her face and said, "Whatever you do Abbie, DON'T CRY! DO NOT CRY!" I felt like a total shit, but Abbie's husband had a good job and made the big bucks. She'd be OK. She would get another job.

...

Abbie told me that she walked into Robert's office, and he asked her to close the door and take a seat. The chair he directed her to was very low and added greatly to her discomfort. This low chair was one of Robert's power trips. His desk chair, of course, was higher so he could look down on whomever the hapless person was who was seated there. We all dreaded that chair.

For the next fifteen minutes Robert railed about how this mistake was not only an embarrassment for the agency but the agency was also going to have to eat the cost of the ad, fifty thousand dollars! Fifty thousand dollars.

This cock-up put him, Robert, in the hot seat because he was going to have to explain to management how something this stupid could have happened, and this was not something he relished doing.

Finally, winding down, he said, "I know you graduated with honors from your college, but you know, Abbie, you could spend a bundle of money and three more years and get a master's degree from one of those prestigious Ivy League business schools, but I doubt you would learn any more than you just did today. I am certain you will never make this mistake again. Am I right?"

Before Abbie could agree, Robert continued, "Everybody who signed off on that ad, and that includes your partner Dennis, the client, the account team, the production department, the traffic manager, not to mention myself, and especially myself, had the opportunity to catch that mistake, and we didn't. But none of them, not a single one had the guts to say it was his or her fault. You were the only person who was honest enough to step up and take responsibility. And in this business, that is as scarce as hens' teeth. So while I could very well fire you for making this mistake, instead I am going to recognize your honesty and integrity."

Robert handed Abbie an envelope and said, "Here's a small check as a reward for all the great work you have been doing. We're very lucky to have you on our team. Now get back to work while I call the boss upstairs and explain why this will never happen again."

...

When Abbie finally came out of Robert's office after what seemed an eternity, the entire department was waiting outside the door to offer condolences.

Abbie looked solemnly at each and every one of us. Especially, I think, at Ellen Blunt.

Then she smiled that winning smile of hers and said, "I'm still here!" Then laughing she said to me, "C'mon, Dennis, let's go. We've got work to do."

Tours *to the* Trouble Spots *of the* World

THE COVID-19 PANDEMIC that kept pretty-much everybody at home in 2020 was a disaster for travel agents. The disaster began with the nightmarish Covid-19-infected pleasure cruise ships that quickly became death ships with passengers trapped on board and no way to escape.

Then came severe travel restrictions, and air travel was almost entirely shut down.

And really, who in his or her right mind would want to sit cheek by jowl on a flight to anywhere during which many of the passengers might refuse to wear masks?

And if you did not already know this: the air you breathe when you are flying is not fresh. It recirculates throughout the cabin. So, if someone is transmitting Covid at the front of the plane, their infected breath is being pumped throughout the plane, even to you in your seat, although you might be wearing your mask, and sitting near the rear of the plane.

So it was a surprise to all their friends and associates when Ethyl and Jake Golden, who had retired from the public relations business nearly a decade ago and were now well into their 70s, decided on a hunch to buy out their local travel agency. They did not know it at the time, but Jake would later joke, it was a Golden opportunity.

...

Ethyl and Jake were unique among travel agents: they absolutely hated to travel. Driving into town to go to Costco was their idea of a long trip. But what they lacked in ports o' call checked off, they made up for with their knowledge of public relations and marketing skills.

They started out by changing the name of their agency to Fly By Night Travel, and their tag line was "Travel Light - Fly by Night." They were able to get the best fares for their clients because they only booked off-hour, late-night flights.

Jake, who was the visual guy, came up with the logo: a large yellow moon with dark silhouettes of three palm trees and a Boeing 737. Ethyl and Jake's grandson, Marty, was a wiz with computers and designed a fully functional website so visitors could book flights and make hotel reservations online. Marty also set the business up with a Facebook page and said he could help Ethyl and Jake beam specific ads to precisely their target market, almost down to the block in their neighborhood. And since nobody actually came into a travel agency any more, they bought out their lease and closed down the office.

...

They started out by targeting seniors with their "Fly By

Night Nightly Specials." Flying by night is not only a tremendous savings, they told their customers, the planes are also less crowded, hence safer, and you can sleep and arrive at your destination refreshed. Ethyl, whose specialty was copy, wrote the words and Jake designed the ads using the big logo and "Fly By Night Nightly Specials" for the headline. Plus four or five examples of flight deals you could not say no to.

The campaign succeeded, and Fly By Night Travel took off, slowly at first, but then it rapidly gained altitude.

...

Ethyl and Jake discussed cruises. The cruise industry had taken a huge hit due to the pandemic, so the cruise line operators were falling all over themselves to provide the best prices. Ethyl came up with the headline for this promotion, "Great News! It's Time to Cruise!" with the subhead, "Score the Best Deal with our SOPH Specials," SOPH standing for the less-desirable cabins (Starboard Out Port Home). It was brilliant, and as Ethyl pointed out, you see the same ocean no matter which side of the ship your cabin is on. Do you really want to have the sun blaring into your cabin?

Something Ethyl and Jake discovered is that a luxury cruise might be the last vacation most elderly people took. For one thing, they could now afford it, and for another, what else were they going to spend their last dime on?

It was Jake who had the brilliant idea: why not offer a

special deal for the elderly who were already circling the drain? The money they would spend on the cruise was better spent on something they would enjoy while they were still alive as opposed to a lavish funeral they would not be around to see. To hell with the coffin, and the hearse, and the unctuous funeral home director, and the flowers, and the minister, the exorbitant cost of the funeral itself, and the burial plot, and the headstone. It all added up to a lot of wasted dough. If they died while on the cruise, it was money well spent. After all, you only die once.

Jake suggested a headline, "Take Our Burial at Sea Cruise – What Have You Got to Lose?" along with half-price off on cabins and a full-flag send-off at sea, should one not make it back to port. Ethyl, who was the more sensitive and sensible of the pair, suggested they call it, "The Ultimate Cruise."

"OK," Jake chimed in, "How about we add, 'Take the Ultimate Cruise — It's The Last Cruise You'll Ever Take.' And we can name the different packages: The Titanic, The Poseidon Adventure, The Davey Jones Locker, The Jules Verne, Voyage to the Bottom of the Sea, The Princess Sofia, and The Principessa Mafalda," the last two names inspired by famous maritime disasters.

In spite of the somewhat macabre and insensitive promotion, Ethyl and Jake were pleasantly surprised that The Ultimate Cruise was a big hit. The elderly who signed up appreciated the black humor and confessed it was the only way to go. Of course these cruises needed to be paid for in advance.

...

Next came the Booze Cruise, targeted directly at heavy drinkers of all ages. These cruises were very profitable because the ship never left the berth. Customers who took these cruises spent almost all their time on board at the bar. They never signed up for local tours in the port of call. These cruises could be scheduled for times when the ships were in port for maintenance. As long as the bar was stocked, these travelers were having a high old time, just not on the high seas.

A secondary market that turned out to be just as successful as The Booze Cruises was composed of people who were greatly affected by motion sickness — sea sickness — or people who, not unlike Ethyl and Jake, hated or were actually afraid of travelling. These stationary cruises were called The Home Port Cruise. Large screens were hung on either side of the ship, and videos of endless seas with the occasional cloud were projected onto the screens, to give the effect of an actual sea cruise. There was no price difference between the port and starboard sides of the ship.

Crowds of well-wishers who appeared on the dock during feigned departures and arrivals home were recruited from the local theater groups whose casts were provided box lunches, a macaroon, and small bottles of cheap Champagne. It was a small price for the travel agency to pay for providing an enthusiastic send off or a cheery welcome home.

...

The Muses Cruises were popular among the literary crowd. Various authors who were on the rubber chicken circuit promoting their new books were given SOPH cabins (Starboard Outbound Port Home) plus free access to the all-you-can-eat buffets and were allowed to promote and sell their books. Authors who had fallen from favor or had been dropped by their publishers or agents were invited to host tours as well.

Ethyl and Jake were really raking in the dough. And young Marty had earned enough by being webmaster to pay for his first two years at college.

...

Then came Fly By Night Travel's pièce de résistance, the Tours to the Trouble Spots of the World travel package that combined both sea cruises and air travel. Inspired by the wildly successful The Ultimate Cruise, this cruise took daring (and despairing) tourists to ports of call in such colorful places as Afghanistan, Georgia, Myanmar, Libya, Syria, Somalia, North Korea, Uzbekistan, Yemen, Gaza, and more. Each world conflict in the news became a new destination for the cruise.

Travelers were kitted out with camouflage fatigues and a variety of vests with oversized US flag emblems in front and a large crosshair target on the back. The vests also displayed insulting phrases in a wide variety of languages that offered such taunts as "Go ahead, take your best shot!" and "What a shit-hole country this is!" Or insults to the preva-

lent religious leaders and other inflammatory and provoca-
tive language.

In each of the ports of call, local mercenaries and insur-
rectionists were recruited to lead the travelers through
bombed-out buildings, IED-filled and pot-holed streets, and
sniper kill zones.

The more adventurous participants could camp overnight
inside an active volcano, or swim in rivers rife with piranhas,
or go scuba diving in shark-infested waters while passing out
samples of squid and sushi to the great white sharks.

Baseball with live hand grenades proved a popular pas-
time. There were hikes inside major earthquake faults and
"Oh Say Can You See?" visits to large underground caves —
totally devoid of light of any kind. The tug-o-war in quick-
sand was very popular as was the opportunity to sit atop a
giant redwood tree as it was being cut down (first come,
first served — or severed as Jake joked).

Travelers who made it home safely, and one or two did,
as a reward for their courage were given their choice of a
free, all-expenses-paid Home Port Cruise, or 20 percent off
their next Trouble Spots of the World tour. Ethyl and Jake
knew full well that none of the survivors would want to
spend one minute tied up in port, so the 20 percent off offer
was a sure thing. And all three tourists who survived the
last Tours to the Trouble Spots of the World signed up
immediately for the next tour. This one dedicated to the
despotic regimes of the former Iron Curtain.

...

Marty came up with a winner that proved popular with people of all ages and especially with dysfunctional families: The Lost-at-Sea Lifeboat Tours (self-guided). Travelers were treated to five days and nights of festive cruise ship life with five meals a day, lavish floor shows, the works. Then in the middle of the night, groups of travelers or families were roused from their cabins, directed to and packed into lifeboats with food and water for seven days, a map, shark repellant, sunscreen, a small selection of unsold auto-graphed books from the Muses Cruises and a GPS locator. Happy to say, almost everybody eventually made it back to land, though not all made it in seven days.

...

Condé Nast *Traveler* did an extensive piece on The Ultimate Cruise and highly recommended it for seniors, as did AARP. *National Geographic* wrote a seven-page, lav-ishly illustrated feature on the Lost at Sea Lifeboat Tours. *Soldier of Fortune* magazine heaped praise on the Tours to the Trouble Spots of the World and recommended its mer-cenary readers volunteer to lead future tours. *The London Review of Books* did a one-column feature on the Muses Cruises with a list of future celebrity authors. CNN and CNBC did interviews with Ethyl and Jake Golden that also included their "Director of Marketing," Marty. These might have been bleak times for the travel industry, but they were days of making hay for Fly By Night Travel. What had been a living suddenly became a brand. There was even some talk about a public offering on the NYSE.

...

Ethyl and Jake Golden were called upon to address The National Association of Travel Agents annual convention and drew a standing-room-only crowd. Marty, who by now figured, "Who needs college when I am making the really big bucks?" — Ethyl and Jake had set up a 401k for Marty that was doing surprisingly well — addressed the marketing and social media aspects of Fly By Night Travel.

Ethyl, and Jake, and Marty were sought after and were wined and dined on some of the most exotic cruises because almost single-handedly they had breathed life back into what had been, largely, a dead industry. And the biggest surprise: Ethyl and Jake discovered that they really did love to travel. "Why did we wait so long?" they asked each other.

The travel industry was booming thanks in no small part to Ethyl's, and Jake's, and Marty's quirky concept of travel packages. Because of their success, Fly By Night Travel was selling franchises on the basis of their successful business model, and they now had locations in many major cities in America.

It was only a matter of time and, in just a little under two years, the Fly By Night Travel Company became Fly By Night Travel, LLC, with franchise locations in the major cities around the globe. Ethyl, and Jake, and Marty, as well, were billionaires, and now each of them needed to decide how to enjoy their new-found wealth.

...

So, Ethyl and Jake who had become celebrities and who were now in their eighties, started to travel, and their travels took them all around the world. During their travels at sea, they met some really interesting people — and some not so interesting people as well. One of the couples they met was Bernard Stapleton, a man about Ethyl and Jake's age, and his attractive young granddaughter, or maybe she was his nurse — it turned out she was his wife! — who had had experience in the banking industry, expressed an interest in doing seminars on investing for the days ahead on Fly By Night's all-new Financial News 'n Views Cruises. After his divorce from wife number five, it seemed Bernard could use a little extra cash, or so he implied, to keep wife number six in the lavish lifestyle to which she was accustomed (following the untimely deaths of her previous three husbands).

...

On a sunny November day, when a brisk wind was blowing in from the east, Ethel and Jake, both of whom had failing health, visited their attorney, Arthur Brown, Esq. They had decided to retire for good and transfer full ownership of Fly By Night Travel, LLC, to their not-so-young-anymore grandson and Senior Vice President, Director of Marketing and Technology, Martin Golden, Jr. Marty could take over the sprawling travel business or do with it whatever he pleased. There were no strings attached.

Then in one of the infrequent times they were at home

and dining at their favorite neighborhood restaurant, over a lovely bottle of 1945 Château Mouton Rothschild, Ethyl and Jake had but one last decision to make: would it be The Ultimate Cruise or the Tours to the Trouble Spots of the World package? They could take their time and discuss their options over coffee and dessert.

– AFTERWORD –

This is the first book of fiction I have written. So for starters I want to thank the one or two people out there who, for whatever reason, purchased this book. And especially those of you who read this far.

Odd though this may seem, I have to acknowledge Covid-19 for giving me the time to sit down and create something other than my stereogram images.

Huge thanks to Allison Smith for her incredible editing skills and for letting me know that I had just the right number of commas and then for helping me put them all in the places where they should have been.

Thanks and huge hugs to Mary Carter, my wife and the real writer in the family who patiently listened while I read each story aloud and then generously offered solutions and suggestions that made these stories better.

Lifelong gratitude to Art Center College of Design for giving me the skills to earn a living in advertising and an eye for type design that I put to use in designing this book.

And if I do not thank Sophie and Chloe, our most excellent calico cats, I will never hear the end of it.

– ABOUT THE AUTHOR –

Gary W. Priester graduated from the Art Center College of Design and worked for fifteen years as an advertising art director in Los Angeles, and San Francisco.

For twelve years, Priester and his wife Mary Carter ran The Black Point Group, a graphic design company located in the South of Market district of San Francisco.

For over two decades Priester and Gene Levine have created hidden image 3D stereograms for publication and for advertising and graphic design companies.

Gary W. Priester lives in Placitas, New Mexico in the northern escarpment of the Sandia Mountain Range with his wife Mary Carter and their two cats: Chloe and Sophie.